DRAG ME UP

MANOR DRIVE
BOOK TWO

KATE BAUER

INTRODUCTION

Manor Drive is a secluded street, set atop a cliff and surrounded by forest, a mere twenty minutes outside of the city. The only way to reach it is the steep drive behind the roadside bar, McKinley's Tavern. The steep angle of the road, and its ascent into the woods, seem to be enough to deter the average person from trespassing. It is at the end of the road that you will find a large manor house, shared by likeminded young people... the house lovingly referred to as "Kink Manor."

The neighborhood on the hill used to be a trailer park back in the day, until the local landfill bought them out and forced the residents to leave. However, the company went bankrupt and the landfill covered before the grounds of the property were ever disturbed. For years, it sat empty and abandoned, nature trying to reclaim where homes once stood... until an anonymous buyer snatched it up at auction.

Within months, the road to the left of the hilltop was

revamped into a modern mobile home court, housing a dozen brand new homes. The road to the right, however, became the private drive for the manor house. The house is a newer addition, added only five years ago, shortly after the bar at the bottom of the hill changed ownership.

No one really knows who owns the small neighborhood on top of the hill, nor the bar next to the highway, but one thing is for certain... as long as it's legal, you're expected to let your freak flag fly.

CONTENT WARNING

This book contains graphic depictions/descriptions of
Sexual Assault, homophobic slurs, suicidal ideations and
self harm.

Discretion is advised.

PROLOGUE
FIVE YEARS AGO

BREAKING
NEWS

Daily News

APRIL 23, 2019

LOCAL UNIVERSITY HOCKEY TEAM UNDER INVESTIGATION

The championship hockey team from Tibalt University is in danger of being completely shut down after an incident last month involving an alleged sexual assault against a student from another school. Charges have been filed against six members of the team, including the Captain.

Authorities state the incident occurred at a house owned by a former member of the team, alumnus Andrew Streaker, on the night of March 17 during a celebration for the team ending their regular season with an all time record number of wins. Witnesses state that the level of intoxication by guests at this party was disproportionately high for the number of underage persons present.

Seventeen citations were issued for underage drinking that night, but there is no record of anyone over the age of twenty-one receiving any reprimand for supplying the alcohol.

The incident that prompted the actions against the team are concerning an individual who had zero alcohol in their system according to the toxicology screen at the hospital where they received treatment and evidence was collected for the authorities. Witnesses state that the victim went from being alert to incoherent in a matter of minutes and was carried to an upstairs room where several members of the hockey team entered and locked the door. About twenty minutes later, some said they heard a scream, and a few other students forced their way into the room.

Police were called to the scene and the victim was transported via ambulance to the hospital. At this time, the name of the victim has not been released, nor the full extent of their injuries.
We will update as more information becomes available.

Local University Hockey Team Under Investigation

The championship hockey team from Tibalt University is in danger of being completely shut down after an incident last month involving an alleged sexual assault against a student from another school. Charges have been filed against six members of the team, including the Captain.

Authorities state the incident occurred at a house owned by a former member of the team, alumnus Andrew Streaker, on the night of March 17 during a celebration for the team ending their regular season with an all time record number of wins. Witnesses state that the level of intoxication by guests at this party was disproportionately high for the number of underage persons present.

Seventeen citations were issued for underage drinking that night, but there is no record of anyone over the age of twenty-one receiving any reprimand for supplying the alcohol.

The incident that prompted the actions against the team are concerning an individual who had zero alcohol in their system according to the toxicology screen at the hospital where they received treatment and evidence was collected for the authorities. Witnesses state that the victim went from being alert to incoherent in a matter of minutes and was carried to an upstairs room where several members of the hockey team entered and locked the door. About twenty minutes later, some said they heard a scream, and a few other students forced their way into the room.

Police were called to the scene and the victim was transported via ambulance to the hospital. At this time, the name of the victim has not been released, nor the full extent of their injuries.

We will update as more information becomes available.

BREAKING NEWS

Daily News

JUNE 3, 2019

HOCKEY PROGRAM SUSPENDED

Tibalt University's championship hockey program has been officially suspended under the weight of the allegations against the players, coaches, and alumni involved in the incident three months ago. During the investigation into the alleged sexual assault at a celebratory gathering, officials discovered a trail of evidence indicating illegal substance use, extreme hazing, and bribery of officials.

Following the breaking of the incident, sixteen other victims have come forward with allegations against various members of the team, including former teammates. University administration shut down the program and all staff have been placed on unpaid leave until the investigation is complete.

As for the members of the team, those not named in the incident or the related findings are allowed to remain enrolled at the school, but are put on disciplinary probation. Those who are named are not allowed to set foot on campus or contact any other student or staff member outside of email communication related to their current semester's coursework. If found guilty, they will be expelled from the school and ineligible to attend any affiliated university in the future.

The first of the four trials regarding the incident in March is set to begin on Monday. We will be in the courtroom to bring you all of the information as it becomes available.

Hockey Program Suspended

Tibalt University's championship hockey program has been officially suspended under the weight of the allegations against the players, coaches, and alumni involved in the incident three months ago. During the investigation into the alleged sexual assault at a celebratory gathering, officials discovered a trail of evidence indicating illegal substance use, extreme hazing, and bribery of officials.

Following the breaking of the incident, sixteen other victims have come forward with allegations against various members of the team, including former teammates. University administration shut down the program and all staff have been placed on unpaid leave until the investigation is complete.

As for the members of the team, those not named in the incident or the related findings are allowed to remain enrolled at the school, but are put on disciplinary probation. Those who are named are not allowed to set foot on campus or contact any other student or staff member outside of email communication related to their current semester's coursework. If found guilty, they will be expelled from the school and ineligible to attend any affiliated university in the future.

The first of the four trials regarding the incident in March is set to begin on Monday. We will be in the courtroom to bring you all of the information as it becomes available.

1

ERIC

"Have a good night, Sass!" Stacey's voice calls out from the hallway. Stacey is one of the dayshift bartenders, so she doesn't usually see the worst of what we can get at night. Plus, with her being assigned female at birth and identifying as cisgendered, she doesn't really understand what we go through to have someone recoil when they realize you have a cock between your legs. Nothing kills the mood like finding out your date is actually a dick-phobic bigot, probably so deep in the closet he's found a set of platforms with dead fish in the heel.

I wave absently in the direction of the door while I work on finishing the blending I need to do for my makeup. My look must be *perfection*. I will allow nothing less. The masculine falls away as the woman in the mirror emerges. Eric and all of his problems dissipate with each and every swipe of a brush or sponge across my face.

"Sassy, you're up next," Cleo says as she saunters into

the dressing area, breaking through my thoughts. "We've got you starting out with Britney tonight, since the elder millennial hooligans in the audience wouldn't appreciate the newer stuff. Betty and Cici are doing Gaga and Mariah. We're not touching any songs not old enough to drink tonight."

Cleo Lee DeStarr is my Drag Mother. She brought me in, gave me a job, and showed me how to be my most fabulous self. Outside of the club, he is Clarence Wilson, my frenemy to the extreme. Clarence kind of saved my life by introducing me to Cleo and the world of drag. But it still doesn't mean I have to like him...

Nodding to the queen in the mirror, I pull on my pigtail wig and stand to shimmy my way into the school girl outfit for the number. My makeup is already good enough to pull off two of the five Britney routines I can do, so I'll glam it up for the finale after the second number while the other girls are doing their routines.

Tying the knot in the shirt to reveal my navel, I feel the calm settle into me. Performing is the only way for me to relax these days. The last few months since the trial have been harder than usual, but being on the stage means I'm Sassy... and she doesn't have those memories.

Cleo blows me a kiss, and I flip her off before I flip my hair. I can't help but notice the concern in her eyes, and it pulls me out of the tentative headspace I managed. I force a smile on my face, hoping she doesn't recognize how fake it is. If she pulls me from the rotation tonight, I'm likely to go do something stupid to bury the memories again.

"Break a leg, Sugar," she whispers to me as I sashay out the door to head to the stage.

After my second individual number, I wave to Tyson behind the bar when I come off the stage. I need a fucking drink. Friday nights are generally good nights when it comes to the clientele in the Monarch Room Dance Revue and Gay Club, also known as the Mr. Drag Club. Tonight must be a full moon or something because the tips are flowing like a stream in the Sahara, and the audience is full of dickheads with their borderline bigoted catcalls.

Walking the floor is *not* going to be happening tonight. Most nights, I get a thrill and a much-needed dopamine rush from the cheering and adoration of the crowd. These guys, however, are more likely to send my mood six feet under like Lizzerati's unfortunate bedazzled recorder routine. Malcolm is a fantastic dancer and choreographer, but a musician he is definitely not.

Plopping my slightly padded ass into a folding chair backstage, I grab the battery operated fan off the shelf. I wish I could just go back to the dressing room to change and go trolling, but I still have to do the group number to close out the show. Usually, I would go do a wardrobe change and show off my most fantabulous self for the grand finale. This sea of cocknozzles does not deserve my best after how they've been treating each of us on stage.

"You sticking around to play afterwards or are you

going to head over to Pegasus?" Tyson asks as he sets my usual Sprite with a slice of lime on the shelf. "If you're sticking around, maybe we can..."

I wave hurriedly at him to stop the question before he can fully say it. I've been flirting pretty heavily with the new bartender since he started in October, but I never shit where I eat. He's proven that he is a great mixologist, and I can't fuck things up *again* for the club. The last bartender rage quit during a huge bachelorette shindig after he figured out that I am not the kind of person who will do relationships. I told him we weren't exclusive, but he somehow thought his cock was a magical cure-all for my issues or something. Cleo had to take the stage in order for Nick to tend the bar. The bride was *not* happy that Betty Whiteclaw didn't take the stage.

"I don't mess around with coworkers, Ty-baby," I croon to him, trailing my nails down his very muscular and tantalizing arm.

Don't fuck coworkers, Eric. You can't afford to lose this place, not now.

"As for where I'll be," I glance through the side of the curtain at the edge of the stage and spot Lucky, Spencer, Scott, and Toby cutting their way through the unruly crowd. "My guys just showed up, so I'll be around if you want to hang out a bit. But only as friends."

Tyson isn't fast enough to hide his disappointment before he nods and heads back out to his post behind the bar. Betty staggers off the stage while I'm still staring at the baby gay's ass moving through the crowd.

Part of me really wants to give him a ride he will never forget.

Don't fuck coworkers, Eric.

I know it's a bad idea, but a rather large portion of my brain doesn't give a flying fuck about consequences. Sometimes it really sucks being bipolar with ADHD. Being responsible is getting more and more difficult. I probably should get my meds adjusted again with the recent stress, but I keep forgetting to make the appointment. I'll do it tomorrow.

"...not even worth it to do the finale with this group. They're not gonna settle and they're making the stage downright dangerous with their spills. It's like they are on a mission to get us out of here."

Catching the last bit of Betty's whisper to Cleo, I am shocked. We *always* do the finale. Even if there are no paying customers, we will do the full show. I've never seen Cleo allow less, and I've been working here for almost four years. Hell, I've been coming here for longer, ever since my father ran me out of his house.

"I'm calling it," Cleo announces and pulls out her phone. After tapping a message, she grabs the wireless microphone from the shelf in front of me. Cleo becomes Clarence for a second, twisting her head from side to side. I hear the crack of her neck before she adjusts her posture from black-belt Clarence to her usually regal self and saunters onto the stage in the sudden silence when all the music is killed.

"Ladies, Gentlemen, and everyone in between," Cleo announces from center stage, her voice booming through the sound system. "Unfortunately, our finale performance for tonight will *not* be happening. It's time for our little butterflies to transform yet again, so please return next month for our new show here at the Monarch Room."

Next month?!

I can't take a month without performing! Not now. I need the distraction, especially with the trial bringing it all back to the surface a few months ago.

I race back to the dressing room and rip off my wig. I grab my phone out of my locker with one hand while I rush through tearing away the clothing, padding, and costume jewelry associated with Miss Sassy Frass. I'm leaving the makeup for now since it will work better to keep me anonymous when I pick up some nameless cock to ride for the night.

Kink Manor Queenie:
Going out. Don't wait up.

I hit send on the message to Spencer and turn my phone off before he can reply. Spencer might be my closest and oldest friend, but he would only try to tag along. I don't need the boy scout Daddy with his adorable ace little cock blocking me. I need to get railed hard tonight if I'm facing a month without performing.

"What are you doing, Eric?" Cleo's sugary voice calls out to me as I finish typing my code into the time clock to punch out. "It's only nine o'clock and you're on the schedule until eleven."

"Fuck off, Clarence," I grumble as I turn for the door.

He doesn't get to pull my safety net out from under me and then give me grief. I can find another fucking job if I have to. Hell, I don't even fucking need to work. Flipping him off over my shoulder, I head for my Mini-Cooper and race toward the South Side.

Fuck my meds. Fuck my job. Fuck all the people who claim to give a shit. I'm going to feel alive for a fucking change and to hell with anyone who gets in my way.

2

MATT

I'm officially an old man. Here I am on a Friday night in the middle of March, sitting at my mother's kitchen table, browsing through listings to find an affordable place to live. I missed the deadline for most of the decent housing near the campus, and what is left would put me next-door to my students which would definitely not be conducive for anyone.

When I moved back to the South Hills of Pittsburgh last summer to help my mother with her chemo treatments, it was supposed to be a temporary leave from the university in Boston. I didn't expect to get the job at Wrenshaw University, let alone to enjoy it. Originally, Syl was sold on the lower cost of living to move here, but in the end, her career and family are in Boston while mine are here. We gave it a fighting chance long distance and had even planned on moving into a townhouse near the university at the end of the holidays, but it became glaringly obvious that we aren't each other's forever when she didn't show up at the airport when I was waiting over three hours for her.

I also got screwed over when she neglected to tell me she took her name off the application for the townhouse. As a result, the landlord denied me the house by myself when I didn't go in to fill out a new application. Sylvia canceling the new lease with the landlord behind my back created a clusterfuck for me. I mean, our breakup is about as amicable as one could be in this day and age, so I know it isn't vindictive. She just didn't think about how her decision would affect me. Her friends are blaming me for somehow breaking her heart, and my friends blame her for not bringing me back to Boston. There's a bit of a comment war happening on social media, but she and I are both staying out of it.

DING

I glance at the bottom corner of my laptop instead of getting my phone from the living room. I was skeptical at first if I would like having my phone linked to my computer, but at times like this, it is really convenient.

Jax:
Up 4 drinks?

LMB:
Who is going to be there?

I don't want to deal with drama, and I really need to find a new place pretty much ASAP. I love my mother, but finding out that I no longer had a new place lined up two days before I was moving out of my old one created this necessary discomfort of living in my mother's living room. I'm in my thirties. I'm tired of feeling like a teenager. I want to be able to jack off without worrying that my mother is going to hear or walk in accidently. It happened only once, when I was sixteen, but that was enough for me to be overly paranoid about it.

> **Jax:**
> Guys from work. Few friends u don't know.
>
> My little bro and a couple of his guys.

> **LMB:**
> Where?

> **Jax:**
> Pegasus

I hadn't been drinking in Pittsburgh since I was fresh out of undergrad so I look up the bar. It's not one I am familiar with. The search results show me that this Pegasus is a gay club. Sorry, LGBTQ friendly establishment. I am almost painfully straight, much to a few of my students' dismay up in Boston, so I wonder why the fuck my friend is inviting me out to such a place. Last I knew, Jackson only dated women.

> **LMB:**
> Not sure that's my place.

I can't exactly pinpoint why I don't feel comfortable going to a place like that. I don't have an issue with people who identify as members of that community, but I also don't feel like *I* belong in their spaces. Being an ally doesn't mean I get to infiltrate their safe spaces. As an educator, I need to make sure I keep my image clean so that I can be where I need to be to make the most impact. And I really don't want to be seen as being dismissive or being intrusive by going there when I am a straight white guy.

Jax:
It's a decent club.

$$ drinks on Friday nights.

U need drinks n ur cock hoovered

LMB:
Pretty sure my cock needs a pussy to be up for sucking

Jax:
a mouth is a mouth. U coming or not? At least come get fucked up if u don't wanna get fucked.

Looking at my computer screen, I realize that it's nine o'clock and there's nothing that will change on the listings before Monday morning. Getting a few drinks couldn't hurt, and at least I won't have to worry about falling for anyone at *this* bar. I am already regretting sending the text about "pussy" to my friend. It's just so easy to fall back into how we were as kids when I'm hanging out with Jackson.

LMB:
If I'm getting fucked up you need to
come get me

Jax:
cya in 15

3

ERIC

Prowling for cock is easier when my emotions are under control. I know I shouldn't take my meds with alcohol, but I just want to forget everything. I want to drown in alcohol, drugs, and dick – preferably one attached to a rich and handsome prince who will take me away from everything to spoil me and pamper me and make me his queen.

How I wish I had the ability to manifest my imaginations into reality. My imagination is probably the only part of my brain that *doesn't* malfunction.

> *Little faggot wants to choke on my cock.*
> *See? He's gagging for it...*

Fuck!

The DJ just put on one of the songs that was playing that night. I guess I need to add another trigger to the list. So far, the weirdest ones are root beer, middle seats, and that gods-damned hockey funk. I have about a dozen songs on the list at this point. I don't know if they were playing during *it* or if it was just at the party in general, but they bring the memories forward, especially this time of year.

I need a drink. I need to fucking forget.

At the bar, I get the attention of Sandy, one of my favorite bartenders here. Judging by the skirt, I am pretty sure they are repping the feminine tonight, but until I confirm I won't misgender them, not even in my head.

"Your usual, hun?" Sandy asks as they turn for the nozzle to pour me a Sprite with lime, but I shake my head and reach for their hand to stop them. I want, no NEED, alcohol tonight.

"Vodka tonic tonight, sweetheart," I say before they can ask. "And I love the skirt. Going with she-her tonight or staying androgynous?"

Changing the subject is something I've gotten to be a bit of an expert with. People can get all up in your business and try to play the game of pretending to care if you say too much about yourself. Sandy just giggles and nods while she prepares my drink. She knows I don't usually drink, but she won't judge me for it. I think she just assumes I'm always driving.

Taking the first sip, I relish the smooth burn of the alcohol. It's been almost a year since I've had any, and *that* was under the watchful eyes of my housemates. It was Shiloh's twenty first birthday and we all celebrated with the timid little kitten in our basement oasis. Eli cut me off after two shots, which was fine because my meds can react in funny ways with alcohol. That is why I got the hotel room and walked over to the club. I'm not risking driving tonight. I might not give a shit what happens to me most days, but I refuse to be the reason someone else gets hurt or worse.

Speaking of Eli, the devil just walked in the fucking door with Jace and my college roommate Steve. He and Jen live in the trailer park across the street from our house. It's bad enough he is the de facto mechanic for all of our cars. Why do I have to see him today of all days?

Jace sees me and sends me a smile from across the room. It would be hard not to see the giant teddy bear since he towers over pretty much everyone in every room he enters. I send him a genuine smile and tiny wave in response, hoping he understands that I don't mean anything by it when I avoid them all night. He may be a large man, but he is the gentlest soul I have ever met. I will shank a ho if he is ever hurt in any way.

"Hey sexy," a nasally voice comes from behind me. Turning around, I see a passably attractive man. I let my eyes take in his appearance. He isn't drop dead or anything, but I can work with it. Six foot-ish with a football player's build is decent enough. The ish is because I can tell his shoes have lifts. *That* is rather disappointing actually.

I stand there and let my eyes take in more of Mr. Wannabe's appearance while he drones on about what he wants to do to me. Way too much hair product with a receding hairline. Shirt looks like it's not only two sizes too small but holds some questionable stains that flash as the blacklight swings over us. What was once chiseled abs looks like the start of a beer gut as he relaxes his posture now that he thinks he has me.

The man is a has-been and is trying to still play up what he used to be. He screams closeted and married, and that is one line I refuse to cross. I saw enough of my father's mistresses flouncing through the house growing up that I would never do that to another person. At least my father had the decency to divorce his first wife and marry the one he knocked up. If you ask me, Michelle was the lucky one in that whole scenario.

"Thought you worked until eleven tonight?" Eli interrupts, forcing Mister Has-Been to take a step back. Judging by the look on his face, the guy has jumped to the conclusion that Eli is my boyfriend and that we are about to get into a fight. The fucking sadist doesn't even try to clear things up and just waves the guy away.

Fucking perfect. Not only do I not get my distraction, now I have to deal with a babysitter all night. Rounding on Eli, I explode.

"Do you even know what the fuck you've done?" I yell at him, making him recoil. "The show is on hiatus for a month. I came here to get fucking *laid* since that is the only other fucking thing I have to look forward to without the club. Unless you're going to stuff me like the high speed train in Tokyo, get the fuck lost, Eli."

"Dude, first of all, you are like a brother to me, so um, no. Second, I can smell the liquor on your breath. You aren't supposed to drink on your medication. You promised to have one of us with you if you felt the need to. I'm not leaving your side if you intend to drink tonight. How would I explain that to Lucky?"

Pushing Eli away, I wave Sandy over so I can close out my tab. It's a low blow bringing the little into this, and he knows it. I can't do this with him here tonight. I'm going to have to find another bar, another club, another life. I need my nameless, faceless dick for the night and that won't be happening with him hovering.

"Fuck you!" I spit at him after dropping bills on the bar top for Sandy. "You are not my father. You are not my keeper. I scraped myself back together over the last five years through sheer force of will only to have it thrown back in my face over the last five months. Every time I think I might be moving past it again, someone shoves it back in my face."

Pushing Eli back, I don't even know what I'm saying as I continue to create a scene.

"I left Mr. Drag because I didn't want to see the damn pity on my roommates' faces. I'm not going to deal with it here either. I think I'm entitled to a fucking drink when I find out I lost the only peace I can manage in order to forget for a few fucking hours a week."

I see the others starting to make their way over, and the look of pity on Steve's face is the final nail in the coffin. When Eli reaches for me, I slap his hand away and run for the doors. I almost achieved it. I almost reached oblivion before that damned Sadist interfered.

4

MATT

As Jax crosses the Hot Metal Bridge to take us to the South Side, I flash back to my early twenties, to the summer nights I wish never happened when I came back home after graduating with my bachelor's degree. I spent more time than usual at the bars and clubs around the city, often doing stupid shit like driving drunk or falling asleep hugging a toilet somewhere. Since I couldn't stay with her on the Mendleton's property, Mom never knew where I stayed most nights. She never knew about the deal I made with her boss in exchange for their "generosity".

"Hey, Prof," Jax's voice cuts into my thoughts, making me jump a bit. "We're here. I'm splurging for valet to avoid an accidental drunk by pissing."

Laughing, I climb out of the car and realize we're in front of a building that in no way shape or form screams club, let alone a LGBTQ club. The drab exterior looks like the bank where Mr. Banks worked in Mary Poppins. At my raised eyebrow, Jax just chuckles and pulls me to the door. The bouncer doesn't even ask to see our identification and waves us inside to pay the cover fee.

Fuck, I feel old.

The sound of the music pounds into my brain, and I can already feel a headache forming. It has been years since I have gone out to any sort of club. Most of the time, I prefer either a chill neighborhood bar or some sort of a show. Syl and I regularly enjoyed a dinner cabaret show in Salem, but I haven't even looked for one of those here. Maybe the breakup is hitting me harder than I thought?

"This is my old high school buddy, Matt," Jax is telling the shorter guy in front of us. I would put him around five eight or nine if I had to guess. He is about the same height as Sylvia. Damn, I have to get her out of my head tonight.

"Hey, Matt. I'm Eli," the guy says and offers his hand. "Jackson's brother is one of my roommates, so I've gotten to know him pretty well. You just visiting or...?"

His question trails off as his eyes focus on something over my shoulder. I turn to follow his gaze and the only thing I can see is a couple of people speaking at the bar. The one guy is the typical jock type, stocky and looks like he couldn't add two and two. The other person is probably the most gorgeous being I have ever laid eyes on. I can't tell if they are a man or a woman, but my dick apparently doesn't care. I feel it start to take notice, so I quickly turn away.

I'm not gay, bi, pan, or anything other than straight. I've never felt attraction towards a guy. Logically, that means the person must be a woman, right? Science says there is a difference in pheromones or something with the hormones.

Yeah, I'm going to go with science and say they are a woman because my dick perking up for anyone else is just too much for my sober brain to process right now.

"Excuse me," Eli pats me on the shoulder as he stalks past me up to the couple at the bar. When he reaches them, he sends the jock away with a glare to start arguing with the other person. Part of me wants to go over and intervene, but Jax pulls my attention back to him and the extremely tall man beside him. It's almost comical seeing the two side by side. Jackson swears he is five seven, but I say that's when he's on his tip toes. There is well over a foot difference in the height of these two men.

"Matt, this is my little brother Jace. Remember him?"

I look up at the man in front of me and it takes a few seconds to see past the giant to the tiny shy boy I could recall from when we were younger. Jace was always small for his age and from what I understood, bullied pretty badly before he was brought to the Franklin household. Never in a million years did I foresee that little Jace Franklin would be this hulking man standing before me.

"I don't think I can call you Squirt anymore," I chuckle as I pull him in for a hug. One thing I've never forgotten about Jace is that he loves hugs.

Stepping back, the boy I remember is closer to the surface as he gives me a small smile from behind his bushy beard. "You can still call me Squirt," he mumbles barely audible over the music. "I like that you remember me when I was still tiny. I like remembering those days with you guys."

He slides a shy glance toward his oblivious older brother as I reach up to ruffle his hair on the top of his head, or at least what I could reach of it. Over half a foot difference in height makes it a lot more difficult. Now I understand how Syl felt doing this to me.

And there I go again...

I need to fucking forget the fact that my fiancée dumped my ass and made me homeless without warning and is now letting her friends villainize me online.

"Let's get some drinks in our systems, boys," I tell them and turn toward the bar. Eli is leaning against it with his head in his hands. The mystery person is nowhere to be seen, so I take it their argument was not productive. Signaling for the bartender, I decide that I'm going to just let it all go tonight. Worry about an apartment, my failure of a love life, and everything else can take a backseat for the evening.

"That an ex?" I ask as Eli straightens up to rejoin us. He shakes his head and glances toward the door with a sad expression.

"A friend," he tells me as he pats Jace's shoulder. "I'll talk to him tomorrow when he cools off."

It's obvious they all know the mystery cutie and are

worried about them. I place the shots I ordered in front of my friends, new and old, and decide we all just need to let loose for a bit. Professor Barnes needs a fucking break, and I need to not sucker punch Eli for upsetting that gorgeous person.

5

MATT

Waking up on Jackson's couch is something I haven't done since before I moved to Boston, but the vibrating weight on my chest makes up for it. I crack open my eyes to see his adorable tortie queen, Bella, staring right back at me. As soon as she knows her minion is awake, her purring intensifies as she starts to knead at my naked flesh.

Wait a second... naked?

Shooting up, I displace Bella and receive a slight scratch and a disgruntled yowl for my disrespect. I pull the blanket away from my lap and am relieved to find that I am at least still in my underwear. Lord only knows what could be living inside of Jackson's couch with the crazy parties that this piece of junk has seen. This thing could honestly be older than we are.

It takes me a few minutes to locate my clothes from last night since someone threw them in the wash for some reason. Most of the night is a bit fuzzy. Okay, it is a lot fuzzy. I remember two rounds of shots and a lot of heavy whispers between little Jace and Eli before they loosened up. We started dancing, and then it goes blank.

A knock at the door has me pausing with only one leg in my pants. Jax won't hear a knock that soft, so I just keep quiet hoping they will just go away, whoever they are. One good thing about his living in this trailer is the fact that there are no more shared walls. His neighbors at the apartment he used to rent were loud as fuck all day, every day. And the lady upstairs liked to run her sweeper at three in the morning.

I'm still bent over with my ass toward the front door when I hear a chuckle behind me.

"Now that is a sight I did not expect to see this morning," Eli says while I grab onto the dryer to keep from faceplanting when I trip over my own pants in my rush to pull them up.

"Jackson still asleep?"

I turn around as I fasten my belt and nod my chin toward the bedroom. Eli hands me a travel mug of what smells like the best coffee ever and turns for the door at the end of the short hallway. Setting down the mug of liquid ambrosia, I pull my button down out of the dryer and over my shoulders. I hear a grunt come from Jackson, whether it is pain or surprise I'm not sure I care, but right now I'm focused on trying to locate my undershirt. Digging through the other clothing in the laundry area, I can't seem to find it.

"Dude, your shirt was a lost cause after that twink puked on it," Jax mumbles with a yawn as he comes out of his room. Of course, the little shit is wearing the same pajama bottoms he wore back in high school. The guy hasn't grown since the eighth grade.

"Your button down and jeans weren't too bad, but we used my knife to cut off your undershirt so it wouldn't get in your hair. Don't you remember?"

I vaguely recall trying to help someone to the bathroom and the car ride home with my head practically hanging out the window. Bits and pieces are starting to come back to me, but I have never had this much trouble remembering before.

"It's hell getting old, isn't it?" Eli says as he squeezes past us to get to the living room. "It's like you hit twenty seven and your body starts to slowly reject everything you reveled in for the last decade."

Jax reaches out to slap the other man who dodges easily. I like to see the banter between them and it makes me really miss the friendships I had developed back in Boston. Actually, it makes me miss Sylvia. She and I had this kind of camaraderie. I never really got beyond acquaintances within our mutual friend groups though.

Sipping on the coffee provided to me, I watch as the two of them move seamlessly around each other to prepare a horribly greasy breakfast with eggs, bacon, hashbrowns, and as Jax always insists, diced veggies. That man has been obsessed with vegetables since he heard they could help you grow taller when we were in high school.

"So, what are your plans for the day, Matt?" Eli asks

me, placing a plate in front of me on the small island in the kitchen. "Gotta rush home to anyone?"

"Give it a rest, Eli," Jax says as he clambers onto the stool across from me. "Mattie here is as straight as an arrow, and the only people he associates with are his students who are, according to him, off-limits for some reason."

Eli only leans back against the counter with a bark of laughter. "Not looking for me, Jackie-poo. Although, I can understand why Lucky is always in a rush to get to school if the professors look like Matt here. Just trying to get a feel for your buddy here and what kind of complications might follow him here."

I had been trying to tune the two of them out in favor of the delicious food in front of me, but something about what he just said is niggling at the corner of my mind.

"Following me here?"

Eli points to the door with his fork as he swallows before speaking. "The vacant trailer at the back of the lot. You said last night you were looking for a place to get off your mom's couch. I told you all about it somewhere between the bear attempting to crowd surf and the pukey twink. I got in touch with the landlord this morning. You are welcome to it if you want it, but I gotta know by noon so he can place an ad in time to run in the Sunday paper if you don't want it."

I don't even know where the fuck we are at this point, but I know it's only fifteen minutes from my mother's house based on how long it took Jax to pick me up. Plus, being neighbors with Jackson and from the looks of it, Eli wouldn't be so bad. And Eli said he's roommates with Jace, so that's another plus for me in the friend category.

"Remind me again what the rent is?" I ask since I don't remember any of the discussions after the second or third round of drinks. If it is reasonable enough, I can jump in easily and if it isn't my cup of tea, I should still be able to get campus housing for next year if it comes to that.

"Well, it is a 1976 single wide model which claims to be a two bedroom, but in reality it is a single bedroom with a laundry room. Because of this, the landlord dropped it from the typical single wide rent. Jackson here pays nine hundred plus the three hundred for the lot fee. The unit you'd be getting would be seven hundred fifty plus the lot fee."

Holy shit. For only a little over a grand a month, I would have my own place. I wouldn't have to share walls, do the small talk in the hallways, deal with a malfunctioning intercom system... none of that. Plus, I wouldn't have to lug my laundry to a dank basement or laundromat each week. I could maybe add a desk in the laundry room and have it be almost an office.

"I'll take it," I practically shout at Eli. He and Jax share a look and bust out laughing.

"I told you his response wouldn't change when he was sober," Jackson gasps out as he tries to get his breathing back under control. "Only person who might be able to change this one's mind is his mom, but she won't."

Chuckling along with the two jokers, we all throw on our shoes so that Eli can show me my new home and get some papers for me to sign. My heart aches as I remember someone else who could change my mind. Unbidden, I recall the last time I even came close to him. I want to remember the little boy he was, not the man his father forced him to become.

Eight Years Ago:

I'm just going to sneak into his room and leave the card. It's the only thing I can do. Mom told me that I was expected at the graduation party, but then I got the email from Mr. Mendleton's attorney. I am allowed on the property for one hour, during which time I am not to approach or speak to anyone but my mother. According to the email, my ban from the property was supposed to be forever and not just while I was in school.

After the fountain incident, Mom finally moved off the grounds. She had invested the excess money from my father's life insurance policy and ended up with enough to buy a modest house about ten minutes away. I wish it was enough for her to retire and leave those assholes in the lurch without her.

"Eric is going to be so happy to see you, Mattie," Mom says as she pulls into her spot behind the garage. She is so excited that I arrived this morning, but I didn't tell her about the time limit. The Mendletons are shit people, but

they pay her well even if she is treated like a second class citizen.

"Heaven forbid the staff cars be visible in any way," I mumble as the car is practically enveloped by foliage.

I'm not quick enough ducking after rolling my eyes and feel the smack of my mother's hand on the back of my head. Turning to the driver's side of the car, I only see the door closing and I race to catch up. If I'm found anywhere but next to my mother today, Mr. Mendleton has already promised to sue me for the cost of my education and the "allowance" he granted me over those four years.

I know I have about twenty minutes until the family gets back to the house after their fancy dinner out with their business associates. Mom is going to set up the snack areas by the pool, but I have volunteered to drag out the cases of pop for the party. It gives me access to the house. It's access I need to drop off the card to explain everything to Eric, why I broke my promise.

After dumping the third case of pop into the steel drum, I tell Mom I'm going to grab the bags of ice from the big freezer in the cellar. None of the staff look my way at all when I head for the servant's stairs. Instead of heading down, I race up to the third floor where Eric's rooms are. That jackass that calls himself a father put his son as far away as possible.

Spilling into the hallway, I look around to make sure I'm in the right place. Gone are the splashes of color and scuff marks that showed a child lived there. Instead, the hall is as cold and dead as the rest of the house.

This is not right. It CAN'T be right.

Eric is vibrant. He's so bright it's dazzling. The sun itself can't hold a candle to him. He isn't this cold and lifeless corridor.

I start throwing open door after door, heart pounding harder and harder, dread rising as I find no evidence of the boy I knew. His playroom has been replaced with a home gym. His "closet" is a guest room. My soul feels like it's shattering with every opened door.

Standing outside of the last door, I am terrified of what I will find inside. Even when the staff managed to clean up the rest of the floor, Eric would never let them clean his room. He had this beautiful chaos about him that could never be tamed in his private space. This can't have changed. It will destroy me.

I squeeze my eyes shut as I push open the door. I don't want to look, but I know I have to. Taking a deep breath, I open my eyes and my heart drops to my feet.

Gray bedspread.

Cream curtains and pillows.

Bookshelves filled with business textbooks.

There is not a single sparkle or piece of glitter anywhere. There is no color, no flair. This can't be Eric's room!

I walk over to the desk to prove to myself that this room must be just another guest room now. I glance at the papers on the desk and choke back a sob. I can see an acceptance letter to the University of Pittsburgh School of Business addressed to Mr. Eric Mendleton.

My breath won't come.

Can a person actually asphyxiate from guilt?

I race into his ensuite bathroom to splash some water on my face. This has to be a dream. My vibrant little man was extinguished by his family. If only I had been there for him...

The sound of tires on the gravel outside tells me I've taken too long to "get ice" and I need to get back down to the party. The last thing I want is for my selfishness to get my mother or one of the other staff in trouble.

Dropping the card I prepared into the trash can in the kitchen, I head back outside to finish getting the party ready. If I can get out of here without having to face the embodiment of my crushing guilt, I will. I know I'm a fucking coward, but I need to remember the boy in the tablecloth ballgown not the man he's been forced to become.

I never did see him at the party. I ran away. I faked an illness and hid on my mother's couch while I booked my ticket back to Boston. I decided to stay away completely. My heart couldn't handle the thought of running into Eric Mendleton, the business tycoon.

"Let's go make it official, neighbor!" Jackson calls to me from outside. "Hurry up, Teach!"

Swallowing my guilt for the zillionth time, I force a smile to go check out my new home and prepare for the next chapter of my life.

6

ERIC

Waking up sore after a night out on the town is not that unusual for me. What *is* out of the ordinary is the fact that my face, sides, and arms are sore and it hurts to swallow.

He's gagging for it...

I barely make it to the toilet before the contents of my stomach come rushing up my throat. Leaning back against the vanity cupboard, I try to remember what the fuck I was thinking last night.

I know better than this. It's too close to the anniversary for me to be trying to do oral with a random guy. Hell, most of the time I take it off the table as soon as I introduce myself since I know it will likely trigger a fight or flight response. Most guys are good with handies or skipping to the main event, so it isn't much of an issue usually.

So why the fuck did I swallow a cock last night? And why the fuck am I hurting so much?

Pushing myself off the floor I flush the toilet and move to the sink to splash some water in my mouth to rinse. Glancing at the mirror, I do a double take. My face looks like it became quite cozy with either pavement or a brick wall. And judging by the bruising on my neck, I don't think I intentionally swallowed anything last night.

Lifting up my t-shirt, I can see a few bruises forming on my chest and torso that are suspiciously in the shape of boot prints.

I wasn't fucked last night. I was fucked up.

Going back to the bed, I notice a scrap of paper under my phone on the table. Picking it up, I am surprised to see that someone helped me. Since I can't remember much of last night, I'm more than a bit thankful for the kindness of a random stranger.

Izzy,

I am not sure if you even gave me your real name since the wallet in your pants says your name is Eric, but whatever. I'm sorry I was such a coward and hid when those guys started in on you. You are really nice and fearless and every-thing I wish I could be. Please don't die even though you say you don't care if you do. The world needs you. Your courage saved many others from those monsters and brought closure for others.

Be well and forget me please. Your light shines too brightly for those who need to hide in the shadows.

Sid

Well this answers absolutely nothing for me aside from realizing that I got my ass kicked by some homo-phobic dickwads either before, during, or after getting some from this Sid guy. I'm not sure how me getting beaten to a pulp saved anyone, but the headache that is building now that I'm fully awake makes me want to curl up in a dark room somewhere.

Digging into my backpack, I pull out my pill container for the day and choke down my morning meds dry. I'll grab some coffee on the way home to take care of the hangover, but I know the headache I'm sporting is not from alcohol. If my head is pounding like this, it means I'm at least an hour behind schedule on taking my medication for my brain fuckups... I mean my bipolar disorder. I can miss a single dose, but if it gets to be longer than twenty four hours between doses, my head lets me know.

Last time I missed for two entire days, I was unable to move from under the covers without immobilizing pain. Spencer and Eli had to force feed me my medications for a few days until I evened out again. I swore I would never let myself get that bad again after seeing Shiloh's face when I emerged from my room that morning. Guilt is a wonderful motivator, even if I resent the others for playing dirty.

Throwing all of my things back into my fuck-me bag, I hope I can somehow manage to sneak back into the house without anyone seeing me. It's the downside of living in a house with multiple Daddies and the littles and pets who need reassurances. They keep me centered, but at the same time make me realize just how broken I am. I don't want what they do. I don't want a relationship. I don't want to feel love. I don't want to give someone my heart only for them to not be able to accept when my brain fucks everything up.

The world would be better off without me in it.

That thought circles through my head at least a million times every day. It would be so easy to miss the top stair or forget to stop at a stop sign or take a turn too late. But in all of those scenarios, my actions would have consequences for innocent people. My therapist doesn't like it, but fact is, it's total strangers that keep me from acting on those thoughts. I don't stay alive for myself or my friends. They would be disappointed and sad but would ultimately understand.

I sure as fuck don't care what my family thinks. Hell, I'm pretty sure my father would be grateful that he doesn't have to bury all the news stories. He paid off the judge to rush my name change after the media leaked about me testifying last winter in the trial against Sabrina Carlisle. He didn't want to have his name associated with "that event" again... not like he ever let it get out the first time.

No, I don't worry about people I know. I stay alive for the hypothetical little boy who would find my body at the bottom of the stairwell. I stay alive for the faceless cop or firefighter who is one incident away from facing his own decision like this. I stay alive so that my trauma doesn't become a burden to an unwilling and unrelated person. It is my guilt over the hypothetical consequences of my death that stops me from taking my life.

7

ERIC

Driving home, I sing along at the top of my lungs to the pop songs of the nineties, knowing that the music can never be loud enough to drown out those thoughts telling me to just forget I have brakes. My nerves are completely shot when I get to the hill leading up to the house. I floor it, trying to get home as fast as possible, swerving around a moving truck chugging along halfway up the hill.

I guess the landlord finally approved someone for the last trailer. I knew of at least a dozen people who applied for it, but no one ever got approved. According to Eli, the landlord has his own criteria outside of finances and rental history when it comes to approving applicants. I've never met the man, but he somehow approved me for the manor house without me applying. Clarence says he put in a good word for me, but I think he just wanted to get me off his couch.

Pulling up to the house next to my truck, my Mini is practically hidden. I watch as Eli, Jace, Toby, and Spencer head over to the trailer park as the moving truck clears the top of the hill. It's Saturday afternoon, so Lucky and Shiloh should be at class. Jay should be asleep. That leaves Scott to contend with. Seeing as how he was out last night, there is a good chance he is still asleep or buried in laundry in the basement trying to make up for the lost time. His OCD is nothing if not predictable.

This might be my only chance to get inside, so I grab my bag and make a run for it. Before I can get through the entryway, I crash into someone and knock them down. Looking at the man on the ground, I realize my chances of escaping without questions have plummeted to zero. Lucky is staring at me in horror, tears forming in his eyes.

"Yeah, I know how I look," I whisper to him as I help lift him back onto his feet. "Please don't make a fuss and I'll answer any questions you have in my room."

I should have known Lucky was going to be home when I saw Toby. I forgot that while he and Shiloh have classes together all week, Toby is in the same Saturday biology class as the two of them, so he should have been gone as well. Lucky immediately fires off a text before I can stop him when we get to my room. At my look he blushes and puts his phone away.

"I had to tell Daddy I wasn't going to be helping the new guy move in," he says and moves some of Sassy's dresses out of the way to make room for him to sit on the loveseat. "Jace speaks really highly of the guy and I wanted to see what kind of man person makes our teddy bear smile like that."

I pause while unpacking my bag. Jace is one of the few people who trusts even less than I do, so if *he* says the new guy is good people...

Considering how wound up I am, I can only conclude I did not get lucky last night, and with how my face looks, I'm going to have to make do with toys for at least a few days. Well, unless the new guy is into masks? The soft knock on my door interrupts my train of thought before my libido causes catastrophic side quests for me. Only one person in the house ever knocks that tentatively.

"Come in, Kitty Cat," I call out, keeping my back toward the door. I know what I look like and if I can prevent Shiloh from seeing it and suffering a flashback, I will.

"Toby said you guys weren't answering his calls and I... I g-got worried," the young man mutters as he cracks open the door to my room slowly. "I d-don't want to interrupt or anything, but I had to make sure you know?"

Lucky gets up and pulls him into the room and I want to slap the boy. Lucky has been here for less than a year. He hasn't seen one of Shiloh's meltdowns yet. We are all very careful not to trigger an episode for him if we can help it. Lucky doesn't see it that way, having to suffer through his own episodes thanks to his monster of an ex-wife and her family. He thinks we are babying Shiloh too much.

"Kitten, I don't want to scare you," I tell him before turning around. "I'm alright and it's over, so you need to just breathe it out, alright?"

It's obvious that Shiloh is struggling not to hyperventilate upon seeing my bruises, but Lucky holds tightly to his hands and whispers something that calms him. I don't know what the little shit said, but he needs to share with the class if it can bring our Kitten back from the brink.

"Was it... D-did it... Are th-they..."

I walk over and pull Shiloh into a hug and shush his attempts at questions. I can feel his body shaking in my arms, but he is so much stronger than the broken boy he was when he moved in two years ago.

"They got away," I tell him honestly, even knowing that it will set him on edge. I swore five years ago that I will never lie on things that are important like crimes, infidelity, or fashion. "But I'm alright. Nothing is broken except for my ego. That will teach me to try and pick up a guy at a rando bar."

"I thought you went to Pegasus after work?" Lucky asks as he sits back on the loveseat. Shiloh curls himself into the smaller man's lap somehow like the kitten he is. "That's where the bartender guy said you were going to when I asked where you were at Mister Drag last night."

I nodded at him and plopped down onto my bed like a starfish. Oh how I love my Egyptian cotton sheets and ultra soft mattress topper. There's nothing like sleeping on this cloud every night.

"That was the plan," I tell him pushing myself up on

my elbows. "But then Eli the Emperor decided to try and tell me what I can and can't do with my own fucking life. So I split."

I lay back down and stare at the ceiling of my room. I don't need to be looking at Lucky and Shiloh to see their looks of disappointment. At this point, everyone in the house is well acquainted with my act first, think later side effect of my ADHD.

"I just can't help it," I sigh. "It's like I have an out of body experience when someone tries to tell me I can't do something. No matter what they say or what their reason for it, I *have* to reject it. It's not even a choice and I can't walk back from it until I calm down. But usually by that time, the damage is done trying to prove them wrong."

I feel the bed dip next to my hip and look over to see Shiloh perched warily on the edge of the mattress. He doesn't look at me before taking my hand in both of his and says, "It's never hurt you like this before. This time could have taken you from us."

I sit up to try and reassure him, but he shakes his head violently still staring at a spot on my wall as if he's seeing something that isn't really here.

"No one knew where you were last night," he says with more force than I'm used to hearing from him. "You were assaulted. You were choked out."

I must have made some sound of denial because he levels me with a glare full of guilt and rage that I have never seen from him.

"I'm not a fucking idiot, Eric," he snaps at me causing Lucky to flinch and start typing away on his phone. "I've seen those kinds of bruises before – on myself and others who weren't so f-for-fortunate. You could have f-fucking died last night! Who would have known, huh? We would have just b-been sitting here waiting for you to c-come back to us, never knowing what happened.

"I would wait forever if it meant you came home..."

I watch as the anger in his eyes bleeds away to pain and fear. This is no longer about me. I never knew the extent of what happened to our shy kitten before the incident that brought him to our door, but if it put that look on his face, I don't want to know or for him to ever remember again.

I pull him to me, not caring about the discomfort my ribs are giving me with the added pressure. Shiloh is clinging to me like I'm going to disappear if he lets a single millimeter of space between us. His sobs and screams are almost incoherent, but I recognize one word before he hyperventilates and passes out...

Mama...

I barely have our kitten tucked in under my blankets when I hear what can only be a herd of elephants thundering up the front stairs. I chuckle softly while Lucky crosses the room to open the door, causing a panicked Toby to fall face first onto my shag rug. As our resident little helps the pup to his feet, he doesn't take his eyes off the young man sleeping in my bed.

"His mom?" he asks, brushing his fingertips down

Shiloh's cheek. He glances up at me when I nod before returning his gaze back to the man who obviously holds his heart.

I bask in the excess love radiation pouring from the two of them for a minute before Toby's head shoots up to look at me again. He lunges for me, grabbing my face in both his hands and yanking me in every possible direction to get a good look.

"What the fuck happened to you?!" he practically shouts in my face before releasing me and hurrying back to comfort Shiloh who whimpers in response to his tone.

Once our kitten settles back into a peaceful sleep, Toby looks up at me with a rare serious look on his face. "Never mind what happened. You're fine, right? You always just say fine so I don't know why I bother asking."

I nod and he seems to think of something because he rushes over to my vanity and starts grabbing random things. I hurry to stop him from destroying over a thousand dollars worth of beauty products and hear what he is mumbling, "Gotta cover it up before the other guys come back over. The professor didn't have as much shit as expected so it won't take that long to unload..."

Snatching my good blending sponge out of the pup's grasp, I push him aside and take a seat. It's not a bad idea to try and cover up as much as I can just in case, but I wasn't planning on leaving my room for the rest of the day.

"This is just precautionary," I tell the men who are smirking at me as I begin my full facial routine. They've listened to many a rant about fashion and celebrity gossip while I've done this on practically any other day. My makeup mirror is my soap box, and my audience is always enraptured. As I feel the soft bristles of the brush glide across my cheek, my soul feels lighter than it has since before the show last night. My makeup, my mask, is my freedom.

8

MATT

Mom took it better than I did when I called to tell her I found a place this morning. I told her I would wait until she was back from her girls' weekend to move out, but she insisted that I pack my shit and get a life as soon as possible. Her words, not mine. I guess my thirty something ass is cramping her style living at home.

When we got to my mother's house, Jackson and Eli helped me pack my meager belongings from the house into my Elantra and then followed me to rent a moving truck. I wanted the smallest size they carry because I honestly don't have all that much stuff in my storage locker. I never bothered to buy much more than a futon and a bed when it came to big furniture because I figured Sylvia would be bringing the stuff from our apartment in Boston when she moved down. Unfortunately for me, they only had the mid-size truck available, the one with enough space to pack up a small house apparently.

"I think it's going to be a tight squeeze to fit it all,"

Jackson laughs out when I pull up the rolling door on my storage unit. Most of the unit is taken up by the pieces of my king size storage bed and dresser. My bedroom is the one area I refuse to cut corners in. I'll have milk crates for chairs, but if I'm getting a bed, it is top of the line.

"I told you I didn't need the big truck," I mumble as I start grabbing the boxes and smaller items to load up while Eli and Jackson continue to crack jokes about how my style is bachelor chic or something.

"Oh my God, can you imagine what Sassy would say about this stuff?" Jax says as he pulls out a framed piece of art that hasn't been on a wall since before I met Sylvia. It was one of Eric's sixth grade art class projects and his mother threw it in the trash right in front of him. He was so proud of the "A" he received on it, and rightly so. I've had art majors compliment me on such a unique find over the years, but for me it reminds me of that little boy's electric smile. I will never forget the look on his face when he saw it hanging on the wall of my bedroom. It was one of the last times I got to see him smile.

Yanking the frame out of his hands, I place it carefully into my car. I'm not going to hide it away anymore, but I don't trust my idiot friend to not break it accidentally. Coming back to the unit, I see that Eli and Jackson finished packing the truck and are waiting on me to head out to the trailer.

"I sent out a message in the kink manor group chat asking for helpers before we got here," Eli says as he steps up to climb into the cab of the truck. "If everyone shows, this will take maybe fifteen whole minutes to unload."

Laughing, he pulls the door shut and starts the truck. Jackson pulls out in front and Eli follows him. I wave them off and head into the office to fill out the paperwork to cancel my lease of the storage unit. After about forty five minutes of unnecessary sales pitches to try and convince me to keep renting an empty unit, I finally am able to head toward my new home.

As I make the turn at the top of the hill to head into the trailer park, I see a man who looks like one of my students racing across the grass toward the big manor house on the other side of the street. That is where Eli and Jace live with a few other people according to the brief rundown they gave me on the ride back to my mom's house this morning. I guess that is another one of their roommates.

Pulling into the small driveway behind the trailer, I see a handful of guys going in and out of the unit while a couple of others are handing them things from the truck. When I approach, I can see that everything is pretty much out of the truck but my seventy inch flatscreen. I'm about to jump in and help when Jace runs over and grabs it by himself to carry inside.

Since the truck is empty, I turn back to my car and start pulling things out of there. A tap on my shoulder has me turning around and I'm greeted by a man who could play a live action Kronk. His whole look screams muscle for hire. I'm not a tiny guy, but on looks alone, this guy could probably squash me like a bug.

"I'm Theo," he says and holds out his hand for me to shake. "Clarence and Eli sent me and Ash out here to help with the stuff from the car while they put together your bed."

I look behind the mountain whose hand I'm shaking to see a person behind him wave exuberantly with a bright smile on their face.

"I'm Ash," they say pointing to their chest. "He, she, they, whatever I'm feeling on any given day if you're wondering. Today started off a "he" day, but with all the sweaty men surrounding me, I might be shifting to they."

He fans himself dramatically while gawking at Theo's backside as he is pulling my suitcases from the trunk of my car. "Just kidding. It's most definitely a "he" day. A very very *gay* "he" day, but "he" nonetheless. I'm nonbinary, genderqueer, fluid in all ways, whatever word you want to use. I'm very go with the flow about it. Just ask for the pronoun of the day and try not to fuck it up. That's all I ask."

Ash saunters to the other side of my car and starts pulling items from the passenger side of the backseat while I am standing here catching flies in my mouth. Have I ever met someone who is nonbinary before now?

Have I accidentally misgendered someone based on my internal prejudices and stereotypes?

"Close the trap, Teach," Jackson's voice calls out from above me. I look up to see him hanging out of what I believe to be the kitchen window. "Ash does that to everyone when you first meet him. You get used to him. He has a pin he wears when he goes out that says to ask for his pronouns. Now come tell us which wall you want to mount your glorious television that I'm going to be conscripting for games on so we can get this party going."

All in all, it takes four hours from the time I woke up to be sitting on my futon in my new living room sharing pizza with my new friends. Theo and Clarence both work at a kink club nearby that is apparently also owned by the landlord of this place. Theo is security while Clarence works reception. Ash is a bartender there as well as working with Jace and Eli at the small bar at the bottom of the hill. Clarence is also apparently a drag queen.

"Come see the show tonight," he insists as he snags the last piece of bacon and mushroom pizza. "It should be a chill night since I took the planned shows off the rotation for the month."

Eli and his roommate Spencer stop talking and snap their gazes to Clarence when he says that.

"What do you mean no planned shows for the *month*?" Spencer asks, looking worried for some reason. "Does *he* know he's not performing for a whole fucking month? And did it have to be *now*? Couldn't it have waited a few weeks?"

While he's firing off questions, Eli is hurriedly cleaning up their mess and gathering up their things. I'm not sure what the issue is, but it's obvious it bothers them that Clarence made this judgment call. I look at Clarence and see his annoyance shift to something that resembles worry.

"I didn't even think of that when I told him last

night," he says apologetically. "The crowd was so awful, especially to him, and I only thought about keeping my performers safe. Those guys last night were not there for a good reason and I wasn't thinking about anything but upping protections by canceling."

Spencer nods his head as if he understands what Clarence is saying, but Eli just looks pissed.

"Do you have any idea what you set off last night?" he yells as he gets in the taller man's face. "He was drinking! He was at Pegasus, by himself, drinking alcohol and flirting with a married man. Whatever happened at Mister Drag triggered a full on manic episode!"

He leans back against my kitchen counter, looking torn as he mumbles, "I don't even know if he is fucking alive right now..."

Looking at the clock on my microwave, I decide it might be time to call this little party before things get too serious and I learn things about my new neighbors that I don't want to know.

"I think things got a bit too heavy here for a yay, new neighbor shindig," I say as I head to the fridge to grab the last beer. I'm not usually a drinker and don't keep any in my home since I stopped living with Syl, but one of the guys brought over a case to split between all of us. "It's about dinner time, and if I'm going to go to this club tonight, I need to shower and unpack some clothes and stuff before I go."

Turning to Clarence, I ask, "Show starts at eight, right?" He nods while still watching Eli pacing in my kitchen. "Great, so that gives me a couple hours to get everything together before I go."

Everyone seems to take the hint except for Jackson, Spencer, and Eli. The latter two are whispering heatedly by my fridge, but Jackson flops next to me on the futon and turns on the television.

"Best part about these trailers? All utilities, including internet, are included."

Pulling up Netflix, he starts flipping through the choices on my watchlist, and I hope he doesn't pick something that will screw up my algorithm again. Sylvia wanted to watch the Walking Dead and didn't switch over to her profile and for six months, all I was getting were zombie recommendations.

A text notification chimes from someone's phone, but I ignore it in favor of heading back toward the bedroom to unpack a change of clothes. I don't really mind having people hanging out here, but I don't want to intrude on whatever has them so worried.

"Lucky says he's home and he's not hurt badly," Spencer's voice carries down the hallway. "What constitutes badly and why did he have to add that on to his text message? I swear that boy has been gearing up for a spanking for weeks now."

"I really don't want to know anything about you spanking my nephew, Spence," Eli sighs and I hear the front door open. "At least we know he's alive and home. I'll see if Doc can come by the house in the next week or so for testing if he's not willing to go in to the clinic this time. I fucking hate this time of year."

"Give it a couple weeks," Jackson pipes up as I hear my front door opening. "If he's just starting a manic phase, you're in for a lot more than a single night of drinking. Better to wait for it to pass before you call in Doc. You know the brat will only do something more reckless if you come down on him, right?"

The sound of my door closing has me releasing the breath I was holding. It sounds like their roommate is bipolar. Remembering some of the crazy shit Eric pulled before my mom convinced the doctors to try lithium for him, I hope their friend is at least getting treatment.

9

MATT

I never did make my way to the Monarch Room for the drag show last Saturday. I got a flat tire on River Road and almost had a semi take me out while I tried to change to the spare. I was covered in mud and God only knows what else, so I called that trip a failure.

Midterms are next week and my students are driving me insane. This is the second semester in a row that I have had Tobias Grady in my class, and he is a menace. Last semester, his friend Lucas kept him mostly in line, but this time it's only him. He's not a bad student, just horribly undisciplined. He reminds me of a puppy sometimes, but I'm not sure how a grown man would feel being compared to a dog.

Between the frustrations in class and the uptick in the online drama from Sylvia's friends, I desperately need a break from reality. Glancing at the clock, I wonder if it's too late to catch the show before Mr. Drag, as Ash calls it, turns into a dance club. I'm not in a dancing mood but would love to see a show.

Seven thirty... I should probably text Clarence to find out what time the show starts.

> **LMB:**
> What time is the show tonight? I need to get out and I did promise to give it a shot.

Clarence:
Show starts at 8pm on Saturdays. Can't guarantee it will be any good since we are between scripted and scheduled shows.

Fridays are 7-10 and Saturdays are 8-11 and second Sunday of the month is brunch from 10-2

> **LMB:**
> Do you always write an essay for a one word answer? 😏

Clarence:

🗨️

Come on down teacher man. I'm gonna do a special number for you.

I set my phone down on my cheap Amazon find, no tool assembly, coffee table and head to the bedroom to get changed. Since it's a Saturday and not one where I needed to run errands, I didn't bother putting on real clothes this morning. Untying the drawstring on my favorite Grinch pajama pants, I chuckle as they fall immediately to the ground. The elastic in the waistband has essentially disintegrated over the last decade plus that I have had them.

I remember the day I got them. I was seventeen and it was a couple days before Christmas. I had just gotten my first car, and Mom sent me out to do some shopping for the Mendleton's holiday party. Their decorator had apparently forgotten to get napkins or they were the wrong color or something. Since Mom was busy cooking up a storm, I was sent to pick up the order.

Fifteen Years Ago:

Pulling out of the drive for the monstrosity of a mcmansion that the Mendletons lived in, I crank up my music. My mom hates that I listen to Eminem, but she's a mom. I think on principle alone she has to hate it. But anything is better than hearing that Mariah Carey song for the zillionth time.

Pulling into the parking lot of the store where I need to pick up the napkin order, I realize this is going to be a lot more stressful than I expected. Now, I understand why mom and the rest of the staff chuckled when I said I'd be back in twenty minutes. It's going to take me an hour to find a fucking parking space!

"There's one!" Eric shouts as the little shit pops up from behind me. I slam on the breaks and turn to face the little stowaway. I'm glad I stopped in the bathroom on my way out of the house... Holy fuck...

"What the fuck are you doing back there?!"

"Get the spot, Mattie! Before that grannie beats you to it!" he ignores my question and is pointing fervently at an open spot three spaces in front of us.

Grumbling under my breath, I obediently pull into the spot, earning a glare from the aforementioned granny. Shutting off the ignition, I turn fully in my seat to look at the little shit who nearly gave me a heart attack before I even get to experience more than my hand when it comes to sex.

"You are in deep trouble, little man," I tell him sternly. Watching his expression fall from pure joy to utter despair isn't something I enjoy. I've seen it often enough over the years from the shit his parents have said and done to him. But I know I need to make sure he understands how dangerous what he did is.

"Sneaking off where no one knows where you are," I hold up a finger for each point I make, "Going out without a coat... Hiding in a car... Riding in a car without wearing a seatbelt... Scaring the driver of the car when the car is in motion."

He winces at every finger I raise, and I curse the fact that my mother needs her job or else I would gladly beat the fuck out of his father for what he's done to this beautiful boy.

"This was dangerous, Eric, and I'm never going to be happy that you put yourself in danger regardless of how positive of an outcome you get."

Climbing out of the car, I take a few calming breaths to settle my heartbeat back to normal. Once I'm certain I can handle my emotions and not blow up at him again, I open the back door so he can get out of the car.

"You're not gonna leave me here are you?" he whimpers and any anger I might have held onto evaporates. "I promise I'll just stay in the car like a good boy and wait for you."

Pulling him into a hug, I kiss the top of his head to comfort him.

"Didn't I promise to never leave you behind?" I assure him. "First, we are going to run into the insanity that is Walmart at Christmastime to get you a coat so you're not freezing your ass off. Then, we're going to grab some hot chocolates at that Starbucks over there. And finally, we will get the stupid napkins for your parents' party."

Watching his face shine with his signature brand of effervescent joy is one of my favorite things in this world. Being surrounded by the decorations and holiday music only makes it a more beautiful sight.

"Deal," Eric says as he starts to drag me toward the store. "But you are getting an apology present from me and you're not paying a dime. This is my fault and as a man I have to make up for my mistakes."

Laughing all the way to the front door, I am slightly terrified what this insane little boy is going to come up with as an apology present.

I'm still smiling at the memory as I towel off from my shower. The little shit wouldn't let me see what he picked up for me until we were back in the car heading home. I had called my mom while Eric was in the checkout line so that I could let her know he had snuck out. All in all, we were gone for over four hours, but his parents never even knew he had left the house. They never paid any attention to him unless it was something that could impact their reputation in society.

Shaking my head to clear the darker turn my thoughts were about to take, I pull on my only clean pair of jeans over my generic black boxer briefs. Sylvia always tried to get me to wear something more exciting, but I don't see a point in fancy underwear for men – at least not for me. Throwing on a white undershirt and a light blue button up, I almost look like I'm getting ready for work.

Sighing, I pull on my black utility boots instead of my dress shoes. I untuck and unbutton the shirt and pull my hair out of the tie I use most days to keep it from getting in my way. My hair has just enough curl that if I cut it too short, it sticks up at all angles. I keep it about chin length and pull it back so that it's manageable and presentable without needing to use any type of hair products.

Glancing in the mirror, I realize I'm also sporting some wicked stubble. I'm about to head to the bathroom to shave it off when I realize I will be late if I don't leave now.

Fuck it.

No one is going to care if I have a bit of scruff for watching a show. Plus, it's probably best if I don't try to look too cleaned up or attractive. I don't want to lead anyone on. Sometimes, being the only straight friend in a group is a challenge on my social battery.

10

ERIC

Fr3n3my:
When I said no shows until next month it was for the planned shows.

Fr3n3my:
You missed your shifts last week. You are still expected to make an appearance and walk the floor even if you aren't selected to perform on stage

Fr3n3my:
If you miss tonight, I'm taking you off the schedule and you lose your solos in the next show

Reading the texts from Clarence should make me feel something. I get to perform again. Maybe? This "selected to perform" bullshit is going to need some explanation. But all I feel is numb. My usual look, Miss Sassy Frass, is absolutely flawless and the patrons love her, but I don't have the desire to put on the Sassy mask tonight. She's chipper and friendly and just not what I can manage right now.

Maybe it's time to try out the persona Lucky suggested for me when he first showed up...

I don't even attempt to stop the smirk as I sit down at my vanity to transform from Eric a la roadkill to Bratney Bitch. I have about an hour to get the look I want and get there for the start of the show. The bruises from last Friday are finally faded enough that I don't have to do too many layers of coverup. I finally don't feel like a freak leaving my room. The rest of the guys have apparently accepted the word of the resident subs that I am fine.

I just wish it was really true. It's getting harder and harder to keep pretending. Eric Mendleton is no more. I don't know who I am anymore. So I paint on a character that isn't conflicted. She isn't confused about why her brain and body don't work right. She isn't terrified of waking up in a strange place because someone dared to tell her she couldn't do something.

She is me for the night. As long as I can be her, I won't fuck things up for everyone again.

Three hours later and I'm strutting my stuff around the floor of the Monarch Room while Cleo introduces Lizzerati as the next act. I wasn't aware we were going back to the old way of deciding who would go on with a fucking sign-up sheet backstage. Had I known, I would have brought my ass down here to get glammed up instead of hiding away in my room until the last minute.

Oh well, at least the crowd tonight is better behaved than the last time I was here. Then again, the riffraff is usually turned away on the nights that Theo is on the door. I was surprised to see him since he usually works Saturdays at the club, but Clarence must have missed having his boy toy close by. At least the beefcake knows what I'm looking for when it comes to the clientele.

"Any prospects for me Teddy-boy?" I ask, sliding onto the stool next to the door while he stands outside on the stoop to smoke a cigarette. Technically, he should be ten feet away, but he only lights up when there's no one outside waiting to get in and Cleo is backstage and can't see that he's not at his post.

"You know, my Clare Bear hates that you call me that, right?"

I wave his nonsense away. Of course, I know Clarence hates that I call his boyfriend by cutesy nicknames. It's why I do it after all.

"That old queen needs to remove the stick from his ass. Or maybe you need to put yours up there more often?"

Theo starts hacking up a lung, and I wonder for the umpteenth time why the hell he still has that disgusting habit. I tried it. I was even a pack a day smoker for a few years as a big old middle finger to my father. Then, *that* happened and I couldn't afford food, let alone cigarettes. I never picked it back up, not regularly anyways. Occasionally, I will have the urge strike, but the first hit tastes like licking an ash tray and it's enough to make me stop. And yes, I have actually licked ashes for comparison because my brain is a fucked up place that demands some fucked up things of me sometimes.

"Brat," he chokes out as he puts the cigarette out on the bottom of his shoe and pocketing the butt. At least he doesn't litter.

"It's Bratney Bitch," I say with a flip of my wig. "Or at least that's who I am tonight. So, back to my *quest*-ion, any prospects for me? I'm off in an hour and need to find a good fucking before I lose it on my roomies."

"Speaking of Kink Manor, it looks like most of the gang is here again tonight," he tells me and waves over to their usual table. "I think the new guy from the neighborhood, the professor, is still here somewhere as well, but he said he wasn't staying after the show."

I peer around the room and spot Lucky, Spencer, Eli, Jay, and Scott watching the show and laughing at Lizzerati's antics. Tonight, she is trying out a new operatic act. It's better than her recorder playing, that's for damn sure.

I'm not seeing much that sparks my interest until my gaze reaches the bar. Tyson is flirting like his life depends on it to the point he's looking rather pathetic. Yeah, most nights his tips do depend on it, but his actions are screaming of desperation. Ugh, I'm going to have to save this guy from the overzealous baby gay.

"I'm gonna walk the room," I tell Theo as I head for the bar. "I might cut out early if this is as lively as things are going to get tonight. Boss-man can cut me for all I care at this point."

I notice his confusion, but I have stopped giving a fuck. I don't need this fucking job. I got enough money to live a couple lifetimes. I don't need to be disrespected.

What I need is to get the fuck away from everyone and everything.

My boss is putting me in timeout like I'm a toddler because *he* couldn't be bothered to be clear enough in his explanation last week about the shows. My roommates are fucking stalking me like I'm a walking time bomb. The only time I've had to myself over the past week that was longer than a half an hour is when I'm asleep, and I get the feeling that they're checking up on me then as well.

I *hate* being a prisoner in my own home. I lived it for the first twenty one years of my life. I don't need it now, as an almost twenty six year old.

Fuck...

Tomorrow is my birthday. That means Monday is...

Not going there.

I never get to celebrate my birthday. It's time I push past... *that event*. I'm going to treat myself. I deserve to cut loose for a change,

Decision made, I saunter up to the bar.

"Ty-baby, get me a vodka tonic," I say loud enough to pull his attention from the slightly uncomfortable looking man he was eyeing up. "And give that gentleman a free drink to make up for your pathetic attempts to flirt with someone who is clearly uninterested."

The man turns to me with a nod and my heart stops. Well, not literally, but *hot damn* this man is like Heath Ledger and Karl Urban had a baby and oh my Dolly Parton blessings, I want him.

Now, I understand why Tyson was trying so hard. I

would give my left testicle for a single night with him. Hell, take them both. From his sexy scruff to the hints of muscle under that tight white t-shirt, he is all man. And the hair? Sooooo fucking attractive to see a man wear his hair longer and not pull it into a freaking man bun to go out. The only thing that would top it would be if he wore glasses. I have a thing for guys with glasses. My first crush had crazy hair and glasses, and I guess I never really got over him.

But I'm not going there. Mattie is my distant past. He left me for a good reason. I heard through the salon gossip line with that he got engaged to a nice banker lady or something last year. That news officially crushed my heart, but I didn't have it in me to be sad in front of the girls at the salon. I couldn't risk it getting back to Ms. Sara that I go to the same salon as her. She's the best lady I've ever met. I used to wish she was my mom, too.

"Thanks for the drink," the man says pulling my thoughts away from the only man, well boy, I have ever let into my heart. "I didn't see you up on the stage yet. I was just closing out my tab to head home for the night, but I wouldn't want to miss a performance from someone as beautiful as you."

Be still my fucking heart!

Or rather my libido. He looks like this *AND* he's a smooth talker? I don't know if I can have just a taste and leave it at that with this one.

"Well thank you for the compliment, Sweetie, but I'm not hitting the stage tonight. I was about to head out myself."

Tyson tries to interrupt, but I throw a bar towel at his head. I will not let him fuck this up for me. The man wasn't interested in the young bartender, but there is something in his eyes that makes me want him in ways I have *never* wanted another man.

"Would you like to accompany poor little me back to my hotel room for the evening? Maybe have some coffee... Lewis?" I get his name from reading the credit card slip he's signing. I suggest we meet there while wrapping my hands around his bicep, loving the fact that the strength I feel isn't visible to the naked eye. Although, I certainly hope to see a lot of naked in my near future.

"I think I might enjoy that," he says after only a slight hesitation. "I just have to tell the people I came with that I'm heading out. What hotel are you staying at?"

11

MATT

I didn't bother to correct the cutie when they called me Lewis. I'm not sure why, but having this person call me Lewis feels wrong. I'll have to correct them later if it keeps bothering me. Most of the people in my life for the last eight years or so use my first name. Only the people closest to me call me Matt. Well, now all of my *new* friends do thanks to Jackson, but for a long time, it was only those in my heart that would call me that, even in my dreams.

"I'm heading out," I tell the table as I grab my button up shirt off the back of my chair. "I maybe met someone and want to see where it goes."

I knew it was wishful thinking that I would get away with saying that, but it is the truth. I'm fairly certain the person at the bar is the same one I saw last weekend that disappeared from Pegasus. Up close, I could tell that, physically at least, they were assigned male at birth or are truly physically intersex. I saw the adam's apple when they were talking to me.

Is it confusing as fuck to have your body decide to perk up for someone that you're completely unsure of their gender?

Hell fucking yeah, it's confusing.

But tomorrow is Eric's birthday and I haven't seen him since the fountain incident. It's been almost ten fucking years since I broke my promise to him and lost the second most important person in my life. I guess if anything, having a sexual identity awakening at least serves as a good distraction from the guilt that has been eating me since I moved into my new place.

I send a wave toward the backstage area to say goodbye to Clarence, also known as Cleo Lee DeStarr, Mistress of Ceremonies. The promised act was a comedic strip tease set to Van Halen's Hot for Teacher. Everyone at the table got a good laugh out of that one, except for Spencer's boyfriend who has spent the entire evening coloring and ignoring everything else.

Eli walks outside with me and waves Theo away when the man goes to put out his cigarette to come back inside.

"I thought you're straight?" he asks bluntly walking across the small lot with me. "You do realize the only women in there tonight were the ones dressed as men on stage, right?"

I give him a playful shove as I get to my car. Leaning against the door, I think about what he's saying. I know he doesn't mean it in a hurtful way, but it almost feels like he's rejecting the possibility that I was allowed to change my sexuality.

"Humans have the capacity to grow and learn and change throughout their lives," I say with my teacher voice to not show my surprise anger at his statement. "Is it really that difficult to accept that maybe I always said I was straight because I was never really exposed to anything that challenged that assumption until recently? Does a person have to be constrained into a sexual identity once they identify it to others? Or can it change and expand as the person grows and learns more about themselves?"

I turn to get into the car, but Eli's hand on my elbow stops me. Turning back to face my new friend, he looks contrite.

"I'm sorry," he says sincerely. "Knowing the stories I know, I was a shithead for saying that. I was told by a very smart friend once to not make assumptions when it comes to sexuality and discovery.

"I'm glad you felt open enough to share that with me, Matt. I just don't want to see you get hurt or inadvertently hurt someone else by just experimenting or forcing yourself into a mold you aren't supposed to fit. Just because you are surrounded by the alphabet mafia of sexual and kink identities doesn't mean you have to change who you are to fit in. We will like you for who you are, even if you have to fail Toby."

Laughing, I pull him into a one armed hug. I have to say, it feels really good to know that I've found someone like him to call a friend. Since high school, I haven't really had anyone that I can say with certainty would have called me out like that. My friends in Boston would have either teased me or pretended not to hear it.

"Toby will get the grade he earns," I say as I get into my car. "As for the rest, come on by for dinner tomorrow. You can meet my mom if you want. We're supposed to do lunch. She just got back from her girls' trip and if I don't have a buffer, she will redecorate the entire trailer while chastising me for being so rude as to move while she was away, even though she demanded I do it. You'd really be saving my ass."

"Fine," he huffs out with a laugh before glancing toward the employee parking lot. "You better be making something phenomenal. I'm a picky eater."

I laugh as I close my door, watching him head over to the back of the building. For a man who claims he isn't a Daddy, he certainly has a lot of the tendencies.

Plugging the hotel into the GPS app on my phone, I appreciate the fact that it is located decently close to home. At least if things go well, I have a short drive home in the morning.

I really hope they go well.

12

ERIC

Shit. He saw me.

I don't know why Eli was talking with Lewis, but I certainly hope he wasn't warning him off me. Watching his dark sedan leave the parking lot, I can only hope he's still heading to the hotel. At the very least, he seems like the kind of guy who would turn me down to my face and not ghost me.

What the fuck am I saying? I said like two sentences to the guy and offered to fuck him and he agreed. Nothing about that says "nice guy."

"You're scheduled until eleven again," Eli says as he comes around the corner. "Why are you out of costume and outside?"

The high I had been feeling from meeting Lewis is wiped away by the interrogation I'm facing. All that is left is the anger and pain. Why does this man in front of me think he has the right to manage me? What gives him the gall to think that he can control me?

Yeah, his father is a billionaire. So fucking what.

I'm pretty damn close to that myself at this point. I learned to live off my club earnings during those few years I was cut off, and never stopped living that way. My trust fund was released to me on my last birthday, and in the twelve months since, it's more than doubled through investments.

"You aren't my father, Eli," I snap at him and push off the wall toward my Mini. "I don't have to tell you shit – or him for that matter."

"Eric, we just worry about you. You know when you fuck up your schedule, shit always gets worse. You might not look at the calendar, but I do. I know what tomorrow is, what Monday is..."

I make the mistake of looking at his face. Pain and fear don't belong on Eli's face. He's a fucking Sadist. He is the one who is supposed to inflict the pain. I broke him.

What the fuck did I do?

I bolt for my car and tear the door open. I can hear Eli and now Spencer calling for me, but I slam the car into drive and peal out of the parking lot. I need to get away from them. I need to get out of my head. A good fucking is what I need.

Little faggot loves it so much he's crying for more...

Wiping the tears away before they can ruin my makeup, I wish Mattie never left me. I never would have been at that party if he was there for my birthday.

But what ifs don't change anything. This is today, five

years later. I have a hot guy waiting for me. I will let him use and abuse my hole so that I can forget everything. Lewis will be my temporary fix.

Pulling up to the hotel, I hand my key to the valet as usual. He just smiles at me, knowing he's going to get a phenomenal tip in the morning.

Heading inside, I grab Lewis by the hand and drag him to the elevators. Once we're enclosed in the metal box and ascending to the suite I reserved for tonight, I push him against the side and kiss him as if my life depends on it. The tension in his body is my first warning that when he said he wanted to get to know me better, he meant actually getting to know me.

He was begging for it, flirting and looking like that...

NO!

I'm not going to be like them!

"I- I'm sorry," I stammer as I jump back to the opposite corner. "You didn't consent to that. Oh, God, I'm so fucking sorry."

My heart is beating out of my chest as I watch the shock bleed away from Lewis's face. He gives me a soft smile and holds his hand out toward me when the door opens on my floor.

"Come on, Cutie," he says softly. "I may be new to being with someone other than a woman, but I know that you didn't do anything I wasn't going to want to do once we got into the room."

Taking his hand, I lead him to my suite. Memories

are assaulting me, but the soft steel of his hand holding onto mine is keeping me from drowning. I look at him in confusion when he holds out his other hand to me. He chuckles and pulls the keycard from my hand to let us inside the room.

Confusion and fear battle inside of me while Lewis leads me to the sofa. Sitting down, he pulls me onto his lap, further muddling my head. But this is so different from anything I've ever experienced. The memories, their voices, aren't as loud or demanding.

"Let's try this again," Lewis says as he puts his warm hand on my cheek. Turning me to face him, he captures my lips in a slow and sensual caress. This time, I am the one to freeze. What the fuck is he doing to me?

My body responds even though my brain is short circuiting. I try to ramp things up, but Lewis holds me back with that single fucking hand on my cheek. I may be a bottom, but I've never been a true sub. I don't give control. I don't let others set the pace.

But there is something about the quiet strength Lewis is giving off that makes me want to follow his lead. My head is spinning, but it's all so very different. This is so different, that my body isn't fighting it. My mind is completely befuddled, but I want more.

I. Want. This.

Lewis gently pulls my shirt over my head, breaking the kiss. I can only stare as he removes his own to reveal an absolutely glorious specimen of the male body. I don't know how old he is, but it's obvious he puts in the work to stay in shape. Running my fingers through the soft hair on his chest, I notice a small tattoo over his heart. Leaning closer, I see it is a tiny unicorn surrounded by stars.

It's beautiful.

When I trace the horn of the unicorn, Lewis pulls my hand away. I lift my eyes to his face and see sadness there. I'm not dumb. That tattoo is for someone he loved and isn't around anymore. Is it wrong of me to be jealous after only knowing him for about an hour?

Leaning up, I kiss him to take his mind off whoever that tattoo is for. Call me a petty bitch if you want to, but I'm not having him thinking about anyone but me tonight. This time, Lewis lets me heat the kiss up a bit more, letting me bury my hands in his hair and hold his face to mine. I can't hold back the moan as his fingers brush over my exposed nipples. His hand comes up to my throat to push my chin up. Nibbling on my neck, he gently lays me down on the cushion.

Leaning back, he raises his eyebrow in question. I nod frantically. I don't know what he is planning to do to me, but there isn't a rainbow's chance in a MAGA rally that I'm telling him "No" at this point. Whatever magic this man has, I'm not objecting. My body isn't fighting with my brain for once in my life.

Lewis runs a trail of kisses down my chest, stopping briefly to nuzzle at my navel piercing. On days I work, I keep it simple. It's just a simple amethyst, Mattie's favorite gemstone. Most days, it helps keep me centered, lets me pretend he's still out there somewhere thinking about me. Today, I wish I had worn another one. I don't want to be thinking about anyone else but the beautiful man showing me things I've never known...

"I love amethyst," Lewis mutters as he kisses around my belly button. "It's my favorite stone."

Before the pain of missing Mattie can take root, Lewis moves up to my nipple and puts just the right amount of pressure into his bite to have me arching up off the cushion. I don't even notice that he somehow manages to remove my pants without my knowledge. My brain shut down for a few seconds there, but the next thing I'm aware of, I am being carried to the bedroom, barely covered by my manties and ready for my...

My what?

Oh, fuck it! I don't care what I call him. He's mine.

13

MATT

Waiting in the lobby for the cutie to show up at the hotel, I took advantage of my headstart to do a perfunctory search to figure out what all I needed to know about making sure sex is pleasurable from the male's perspective, as far as receiving goes. I mean, Sylvia and I went through a bit of an experimentation phase where she tried pegging me, so I know I'm not really keen on bottoming. But I want to make sure that I get this right for my cutie.

I really need to figure out their pronouns...

"Mr. Pierce is here again," the valet exclaims, jumping up and racing for the front door. The person who exits the stylish Mini Cooper is none other than my cutie. Mr. Pierce, huh?

"Good evening, Mr. Pierce," the concierge says as he strides into the lobby, but the woman is ignored completely. My cutie grabs my wrist and pulls me into the elevator and begins to show me just how much I wasn't misreading his signals at the bar.

When something spooks him, I take over. I may have never been with a man before, but I have been with nervous subs before getting together with Sylvia. This cutie is desperate to let go and submit, and I will do whatever it takes to get him there.

I spend the next hour slowly gaining his trust with soft kisses and easy touches. There is a bit of a moment where he starts to tense. Something about his belly button ring upset him. I'm not sure what I said or did, but I resolve to avoid the piercing and get us back on track. When I'm certain he is ready, I remove the rest of his clothing and lift him in my arms to bring us to the bedroom.

It's been so long since someone has felt so *right* in my arms. I don't think I've ever felt it when it came to my sexual partners before. There is something special about him.

My cutie whines when I lay him down on the bed and stand up. I chuckle while I remove my jeans and boxer briefs. I didn't comment on his, but I might have to admit Syl that I finally understand the appeal of lace for men. They look amazing on him.

I watch as his hungry eyes take in my naked body. There is a wariness to his gaze, but as he licks his lips, I know he is more eager than anything else. Climbing on the bed next to him, I trace the top edge of his pretty panties with my fingertips and lean in for a kiss.

"You know, I should probably know your name

before we go any further, Cutie," I murmur against his lips as I slide my hand under the scrap of fabric to feel him. I'm not surprised by the moisture or the fact that his skin is silky smooth around his very erect penis.

The sounds he is making help me to understand that I'm doing everything right for him. I never imagined my mother's obsession with romance books would help me in real life, but some of her books are turning into a freaking how-to manual for me right now.

"A name, Cutie?"

He shakes his head back and forth on the pillow while I slowly stroke him under his pretties. When he arches his back, lifting his hips off the bed, I pull my hand away with a chuckle. I want to bring him pleasure, but a part of me really wants to truly connect with him first.

My cutie lets out a groan of frustration as he glares at me. Leaning over him, I plant a kiss on his forehead and lay back on my side next to him, propping myself up on one elbow.

"I need a name, a condom, and some lube if you want to go further, Cutie," I tell him. His glare shifts to a look I can't identify, but he points to the bedside table without saying anything. Opening the drawer, I see a bottle of lube and an unopened box of condoms. Sitting up to fight with the plastic on the box, I notice the brat in the bed giggling silently.

Seriously, what is this plastic made of? They need to make the condoms out of this stuff. Maybe then there wouldn't be so many oops babies.

The giggles behind me turn to full laughter when I am forced to get up and grab my keys out of my jeans pocket to cut the plastic away from the box to get to a damn condom. Lifting a strip in triumph, I jump back on the bed, on top of the brat who isn't even attempting to be contrite for laughing at me. Reaching for his sides, I tickle him until he is breathless and we end up staring at each other's smiling faces like the sun just broke through the clouds.

"Are you alright with bottoming?" I ask him, running my fingers down to the top of his pretties. "If not, we'll have to stick to hands or frotting because I don't think I make a good bottom."

My cutie smiles like I just told him he could have ice cream for dinner for the rest of the year. Pushing my hand away from his undies, he squirms out of them to reveal he is wearing a plug. My dick goes from being ready to barely holding back. I feel a squirt of precum escape and barely stop myself from thrusting when Cutie swipes those few drops to bring to his mouth.

Groaning, I push his legs wide and settle myself kneeling in between. I slowly remove the plug from his ass, too slowly judging by the looks he throws my way. I get a bit of a thrill making him squirm as I slowly fuck him with his toy before I finally pull it free. I tear open a condom with my teeth and roll it carefully onto my dick. I'm a whisper's breath away from blowing, but I refuse to give in until I am inside of this amazing creature.

Adding more lube, I line myself up with his hole and wait until I have eye contact.

"I need a name, Cutie."

Frustration and desperation war in his eyes before his need wins out.

"Call me King."

I try to ease into him slowly, but King takes matters into his own hands, or legs for that matter. Wrapping his ankles behind my back, he surprises me and pulls me into him with a single thrust. It's heaven and hell seeing the pain battling the ecstasy on his face. I didn't want to hurt him, never him. I know I'm not porn star big, but I'm definitely a needs prep type of big.

"Shhh," I whisper as I run my fingers through his short turquoise hair, letting my nails gently scrape against his scalp. "Let your body get used to me. I don't want to hurt you, Cutie."

After a few sniffles on his end, he starts wiggling and I take that as my signal to start slowly rocking in and out of him. Every time he tries to take control and speed us up, I give him a little smack on the hip. Staring into his gorgeous blue eyes, I feel like I've met the other half of my soul. Time stops mattering. The only thing that matters is staying forever connected to this person.

It could have been hours or minutes, but when King's eyes widen in pleasure, I take pride in the way his body arches off the bed and his release coats his chest between us. The rhythmic contractions hugging my dick send me over the edge with him as my whole body tenses. I push my hips into him to get as deep as physically possible.

I never want to separate from this ethereal beauty, and I pray the universe will let me keep him.

14

ERIC

What the fuck did I just do?

My go to name for hookups is not King. Why couldn't I just give him my father's name, like all of the others? Yeah, I get a bit of a kick out of my homophobic father's name being screamed by guys railing my ass. It makes up for the empty feeling I'm always left with.

Except, I'm not feeling empty this morning.

I woke up at my usual escape the fuck-toy time so that I can beat the sun and most of Kink Manor for my walk of shame, but for the first time ever I don't want to just run off.

What Lewis and I did last night wasn't a frenzied one night only fuck-fest to drown out the bad shit. I don't know what it was, but it wasn't frenzied. Nor do I want it to be a one night stand.

Wait...what?

I never want a repeat. Sex on repeat just means they'll expect a relationship. I don't do romance.

But I want to with Lewis...

Slipping out of the bed, I hurry to the couch to get dressed. I can't do this. I can't be like this after only knowing this guy for a few hours and one *fucking phenomenal* night of sex. No... making love.

Shoving my fist in my mouth to hold back the sob that wants to escape, I realize what my problem is. I can't risk hurting him like I hurt everyone else. I have to push him away before he abandons me, or worse, feels obligated to me.

Swallowing the bile that rises in my throat, I grab my fuck-bag from the closet and run from the suite. The elevator ride down to the lobby gives me enough time to gather myself and realize that Lewis at least deserves an explanation. Exiting the elevator, I walk to the front desk and grab a notepad and pen to have a note delivered to him.

"Good Morning, Mr. Pierce," the daytime concierge greets me as usual. "We will have an attendant escort your guest out of the room once you leave as requested. Is there anything else I can do for you this morning or in preparation of your next visit?"

I look up from my note to stare at the man in front of me. Am I really that much of an ass that I've had the guys I've been with woken up and kicked out at the ass crack of dawn? Judging by the bored look on the concierge's face, I am.

"Uh, let this one sleep," I tell him, feeling ashamed at the shock he shows. I hand him the note. "And give him this when he comes down. His name is Lewis."

"We will just slide it under the door, Sir. Not everyone leaves through the lobby."

The man behind the desk is looking at me like I grew a second head, so I hurry out to where the valet has my car waiting for me. Pulling a few bills out of my wallet, I place them in his hand and dive into my car. Based on the fact that he doesn't move as I pull away, I think I might have really over-tipped this time.

Oh well, it's not like I can't afford it. I just won't order takeout this week.

When I pull up at a stoplight, I power on my phone and almost regret it immediately. Text notifications start chiming through the sound system to the point that I can't even enjoy the music softly playing on my system.

Softly?

I glance at the screen and turn the dial to see what number my speakers are on. Twelve?! That's the level I put it when I know someone else is going to be driving so I don't blow out their ear drums. I never have it lower than twenty if it's just me. Somehow, I'm almost home and didn't even notice.

The intrusive thoughts didn't need drowning out.

Not ready to face everyone at the house, I pull in at the Devil, hiding my car in the mix of vehicles from people still playing inside. I know they've stopped letting people in at this point, but they won't be kicking anyone out for at least a half an hour. The workers are done at seven, so they usually give everyone else the boot around six or so.

I chuckle as Seth pokes his head out of the front door

to see who pulled in. I wave his attention away and shake my head when he hikes his thumb behind him, asking if I want to come in. Usually when I show up alone, they will accommodate me no matter the time. I've never before wondered why I get preferential treatment, but I think it's Clarence's way of being nice without being obvious.

Pulling up the text messaging app on my phone, I sigh at the various messages from my friends and roommates and wonder just how bad I've been that they have to follow up with me like this. I need to stop making them worry. Maybe it's time to finally leave Pittsburgh behind and just go where nobody knows me?

> **Lucky:**
> Daddy says you have a baby bi to take care of.
>
> Does this mean I am going to be a big brother now?

I bark out a laugh at the absurdity of my favorite adorable little. I'm really glad that is the first message I decided to open because the others aren't quite as much fun.

> **Sad-die:**
> I know you think you know best but I will have Steve disable your vehicles if you run out on me again

Eli can kiss my lily white ass. If Steve comes anywhere near me or my vehicles this week, someone is going to end up in the fucking hospital. I quickly glance through the rest of my messages so that I know what I'm walking into when I get home.

> **Toby:**
> Did you pop my econ professor's ass cherry?
>
> **BFF Daddy:**
> Eli is pissed.
>
> Kitten is worried. Toby is drunk.
>
> Come home safe.
>
> Lucky says he wants a baby brother? 🙃

Hold up... Toby's Econ professor?

I can vaguely remember something about him from one of Lucky's impromptu "Protect Eric from Dwelling on *That Event* Movie Days" a few months ago.

"You should have seen it," Toby says as he flops down on the pile of cushions. I hate to say it, but the little shit is a welcome distraction. There's no way that Lucky could have known that Mulan was a bad choice for me. I'm fine with the live action, but the song Reflections guts me. It reminds me of my senior year of high school, how I lost who I am completely without my guiding light, my north star, after he disappeared from my life.

"And I mean, he's like probably THE hottest guy on campus. Totally Master material," Toby continues on with his story. "Like remember when he manhandled that

asshole that was all up in your face? This was like that but like a zillion trillion quadrillion times better."

His description definitely intrigues me, but I can't seem to reach deep enough for a genuine smile. Lucky seems invested in the story. Toby is animatedly reenacting some sort of scene with a fight and the professor doing something to break it up.

"And then Professor Barnes legit growled at them," he exclaims before flopping back onto the pile of cushions.

"Barnes?" My heart skips a beat. Could it be? Mattie was always good with numbers.

Toby sits up and nods excitedly. "Yeah, Professor Lewis Barnes. Like he's got the old man name part of a professor, but oomph is he so not an old man."

I hurriedly put the car in reverse and back out of the parking space. I need to get back to the house and get more information from the drunken pup. If Lewis is really that same Professor Barnes, I need to fix this. I can't jeopardize any of the boys' educations because I can't keep my ass to myself. I refuse to let my fuckups hurt the people I love.

15

MATT

Waking up to the sound of the door closing was not how I expected to greet this morning. Falling asleep with King in my arms after we made love was easily in my top three memories of all time. Number one will always be the day Mom introduced me to the family she worked for and I got to meet the little boy who would steal away the biggest chunk of my heart with a single smile. Number two is the last memory I have of my father. I remember him hugging me, telling me how proud he was of me winning the math tournament in second grade.

I thought King felt the same as I do. I'm not sure how much of last night was just my wishful thinking at this point, but I think it's safe to say I'm not straight.

Understatement of the century right there.

Laughing, I half expect a bellboy to be pounding on the door telling me I have to leave now that the person paying for the suite has left. Isn't that the way these things go? Wham. Bam. Thank you, Ma'am... well, Man.

Feeling like shit for being dumb enough to expect feelings from a bar hookup, I hop in the shower to at least feel like I'm getting something worthwhile out of this room. I'd never be able to afford a room in this hotel, let alone a suite, on my salary while I'm still paying off my student loans for my doctorate. Wrenshaw isn't exactly an elite school, but if I can make tenure next year, maybe I could save up for a night at this place after a year or two.

After drying off using some of the softest towels I've ever experienced, I feel a bit grungy pulling on the clothes from last night. My eyes are itchy and dry, but I can't do anything about my contacts until I get home. I don't usually wear them to sleep in, but I left my glasses at the trailer. I wasn't planning on staying out all night. Pulling my hair up to get it out of the way and hopefully prevent a tangled mess, I double check that I have everything.

Keys? Phone? Wallet?

Maybe searching the suite for things I might have left is a good excuse, but I know that I'm searching for a note or something. Something inside of my chest starts to hurt when I realize my cutie didn't leave me anything. I meant nothing to him.

Pulling the covers back on the bed to make sure housekeeping cleans the linens, a scrap of shiny fabric falls to the ground. I feel a bit like a perv putting his panties in my pocket, but I feel like I deserve something to remember this night by.

Dejected, I leave the room and head for the door to

the suite. Before I can turn the handle, an envelope is pushed under the door. It is labeled with my name, so I open it up, praying it's not the bill for the room.

Lewis,

Last night was amazing for me and a one of a kind experience. And since it was one of a kind, I don't want to ruin that memory. Please understand this isn't a reflection on your skills because sweet baby Jesus, you are a sex god. If fate ever brings us back together, I'll take it as a sign.

Thank you,
Your King

Tucking the note into my back pocket, I exit the suite. Not wanting to deal with anyone seeing my walk of shame, I use the stairs to go all the way down to the parking lot, bypassing the lobby. Climbing into my Elantra, I feel horribly out of place surrounded by the brand new Porsches and BMWs. God, he is so out of my league.

I'm a fucking idiot.

I just sit in my car, waiting for the defroster to clear the morning fog from my windshield and wait for my phone to power back on. It must have died on me at some point last night. The sound of the "Hello Moto" echoing through my silent car reminds me that I forgot to turn the radio back to the satellite radio instead of using the Android Auto to stream music.

Picking up my phone, I notice a couple new text messages from the guys I've befriended the last couple of weeks.

Spencer:
Hurt him and I'll bury you

Clarence:
Call me when you get this.

Eli:
Don't make me kill you. I have the connections to make you disappear

Clarence:
The SECOND you get this

Jax:
You should've picked a different starter dick

I'm completely lost as to what is going on. I thought everything was good when I left the club last night, so I hit the button to call Clarence. Wincing at the hour, I hope he's a morning person because the sun is barely over the horizon.

"Thank fuck," he says instead of a greeting. "I thought someone killed you. Not you, Theo. Go back to sleep, babe."

I let out a chuckle as I drop my head back against the

headrest. At least someone out there doesn't want to kill me for some unknown reason.

"Why does everyone suddenly want to kill me?"

Clarence sighs dramatically and I hear rustling noises followed by what sounds like a door closing.

"Do you know who you took home from the bar last night?"

Horror shoots through me. "Fuck. Don't tell me he isn't single."

"No. It's nothing like that," my friend hurries to reassure me. "It's just that he is... Well, he's a bit fragile even if he refuses to admit it. A lot of people love him and worry about him and his decisions when he starts exhibiting certain patterns."

Thinking back on some of the recent conversations I've overheard since moving into the trailer, I have a feeling that I know what the connection is and let out a sigh.

"This is the roommate who is bipolar, isn't it?" I ask, already knowing what his response will be.

"It's more than just that," he tells me as I hear a Keurig in the background. "Are you home? This is going to be more than a phone call if you think you might want more with him. If you're content with just the one night, I have to ask you to pretend it never happened if you see him again."

"I'll be home in about fifteen minutes," I tell him as I pull out of the parking space. "I want forever if he'll have me. I don't know why, but it feels like we're meant to be."

Clarence starts coughing on the other end of the call

and manages to choke out that he will come over as soon as I'm home, so I rush as much as I can to get there. At the top of the hill, I glance over toward the house, hoping to see the Mini parked with the other vehicles. I tell myself it's because I want to make sure he made it home safely, that's all.

When I don't see the car, I feel a tightness in my chest. He left so much earlier than I did. Why isn't he home?

It takes a concentrated effort to turn left into the trailer park and head to the back where my home is. Pulling into my driveway, I notice a few lights get switched off in a hurry in the neighboring trailers. Instead of going in the back door, I walk around to my front door where Clarence is waiting for me with a cup of coffee and a look of pity.

16

MATT

Sitting with Clarence at my little breakfast bar area feels strange without the other guys around, but we both sip our coffees for a few minutes before he takes a deep breath and takes my hand.

"How much do you know about the man you were with last night?"

Taking another sip, I run through everything I actually know for a fact and frown. It's actually very little.

"He told me his name was King, but thinking back on it I'm pretty sure that was a lie," I say as Clarence curses under his breath. "I know the hotel staff called him Mr. Pierce. I know he drives a Mini Cooper. I know he is a stickler for consent."

"That's an understatement," Clarence mutters before he takes another swig of his coffee. "Anything else without getting into the sex stuff? I don't need to know details."

Chuckling, I shake my head.

"And you think you're soul mates or something based on a fake name and a car?"

"Something tells me you know what I'm talking about by the way you and Theo are around each other," I give him a pointed look as I get up to pour a fresh cup from the pot of coffee I started when we came in. "My parents showed me what a true soul connection should be between lovers. I just thought it would never happen for me until last night."

At his questioning look, I tell my friend the epic love story of Sara and Lewis Matthias Barnes, the First. By the time I finish, he's holding his side from laughing and wiping the tears from his eyes.

"Oh, I can't wait to meet them both," he gasps out as he gets up to pour himself another cup.

"You'll probably meet Mom later today when she comes over for lunch," I tell him with a chuckle. "Dad's got a lot farther to travel and I don't think I know any necromancers that could help us out with that."

Clarence pauses putting the carafe back onto the hot plate.

"I... I didn't know. I'm sorry."

I wave his concern away with a smile. "It happened when I was a kid. Damned deer ran out in front of a car in another lane when he was on his way home from a work trip. Cops said the driver swerved to miss the deer but lost control and would've gone through the guardrail and over the cliff. Dad managed to get in the way enough to keep everyone on the road, but his car didn't have side air bags. They just didn't catch the brain bleed in time. I heard them talking about it while my mother was sleeping. The other driver was a young pregnant woman with a toddler in the car, so Dad made the EMTs take care of them first."

Shrugging, I carry my coffee over to the futon and sit. "At the time, I was sad that my father was gone, but he saved that family. My mom knew it too. She would always tell me to hold my head high, that I'm the son of a hero. So don't worry about bringing him up. I'm probably always going to miss him. But I'm proud to be his son and will never shy away from talking about my hero."

Glancing toward the kitchen, I have very little warning before getting tackled in a bear hug.

"I really hope the brat can get over his shit enough to love you back," Clarence whispers in my ear before pulling back. Sitting next to me on the futon, he grabs my hand in both of his and starts to explain what everybody's problem is with me taking King back to the hotel.

"First of all, you're right. He lied to you about his name. I'm honestly surprised that he gave you *that* name when you asked. He usually doesn't respond positively to being called King. It's got some very negative connections with his past, and those who used to call him that would never dream of it now. I would advise you not to use it with any of the other guys in reference to him.

"The Mr. Pierce thing is new, but I'm pretty sure that is his middle name. It makes sense for him to use a false name if he's out and about. Five years ago, something happened that his father spent a shit ton of money to keep his name out of. The man wouldn't take kindly to having it known that his son is taking hookups to a hotel," he chuckles as he reaches for his coffee. "His sperm donor is a fucking asshole. I never got confirmation, but I'm pretty sure his father tried to kill him before he kicked him out."

I'm surprised by the growl that somehow managed to come out in response to that statement. *I'm reading too many of Mom's werewolf romances...*

"That's when he came into my life, though. I found him collapsed on the loading dock of the Monarch Room about five years ago. He was barefoot with his feet torn to shreds and soaked to the bone." Clarence's voice went from teasing to ice cold. "He was ready to die, Matt. His eyes were already there. I'd seen it before in my...

"Let's just say I've seen it before. It was too soon after... after losing someone very dear to me. I couldn't let this beautiful boy leave the world, too.

"I didn't know what I was doing. I brought him inside. I moved him onto my couch. I introduced him to drag in the hopes that it would give him *something* to live for. I tried to be there for him, but I couldn't handle him. It wasn't until after I convinced Eli to move him into the big house that any of us found out that he is bipolar.

"Scott recognized the name of one of the medications that he left in the bathroom. After we got him back on his meds, we all took turns watching over him. I guess we never got out of that habit."

Five years? They have been treating him like a ticking time bomb for five fucking years and yet they wonder why he acts out like this. The fucking audacity of them all.

"Have you ever considered your hovering might make things worse?"

I don't even try to soften the question. After I was forced away from the Mendleton house, I did a lot of research into what is and isn't helpful for someone who is bipolar. A lot of studies seem to be biased to sell a particular drug, but some of the blogs I read over the years from people dealing with the disorder have said that it's important for the person to have a balance of independence and a support system. One without the other can result in more severe episodes of mania or can develop into an anxiety disorder.

I'm pretty sure what his friends did is smother him until the stress of putting on a show broke him, forcing manic episodes bordering on psychotic breaks. I watched it happen with Eric when he was a kid and no one knew what his condition was. I always knew it was more than merely acting out for attention.

"Stress triggers mania. Feeling like you're under constant observation is a hell of a lot of stress, especially for five fucking years."

Clarence looks at me with haunted eyes. "Better stressed and alive than the alternative," he tells me as he heads to the door. "I'll pick up the mug when I come over later if you still want me to come meet your mom."

When the door closes behind him, I drop my head

into my hands and weep for the young man who has been through hell because of his own brain chemistry and well meaning but misguided friends. Pulling the panties and note out of my pockets, I pray for the first time in years that someone will look over this precious young man and bring him some relief.

17

ERIC

I barely remember to put the Mini in Park before I race into the house. I know I'm in a rush to wake up the drunk pup to question his ass, but wrecking my car into the side of the garage would not be a good way to do it – mainly because I don't want to deal with the increase to my insurance premium. The front door slams against the shoe rack in the entry hall, making me wince as I kick my ankle boots in that general direction. I really hope I don't wake everyone up, but my brain is in hyperfocus mode. I need to know what the fuck is going on, who our new neighbor really is. The grumbling and noise coming from up the stairs tells me I was unsuccessful in keeping this between me and the pup, so I head up.

"You are a BAD puppy, Tobias Grady!" I call out as I reach the landing for where most of our bedrooms are. If I'm going to wake everyone up, I might as well do it right.

The door at the end of the hall cracks open to show

Lucky in his footie pajamas rubbing his eyes and sucking on his rainbow binkie. His crochet Asexual flag Mothman is clutched under his arm and he's looking at me like he wants to cry. I send him a smile and do a little fairy wave to make him giggle. I'm not mad at him. I know if he had put it together, he would have told me.

Spencer stomps down the steps from the third floor to come up behind his little boy, looking relieved. But I'm pissed at him as well. Based on his texts, he put it together just like Toby did. Only the difference is Toby doesn't know who "Lewis Barnes", professor of economics, could be to me. Spencer does.

Scott, Jace, and Shiloh come out into the hall while two sets of footsteps come up the stairs behind me. I turn to see Eli and Jay approach with different looks on their faces. Jay looks relieved to see me, but Eli looks guilty as fuck.

Does he know, too?

The only person who isn't here is the one who set me off.

"TOBIAS ANDREW FUCKING GRADY!" I yell and stomp my foot. I feel bad when I see Shiloh wince and run to hide behind Jay and Eli, but my anger rolls right over the shame. I'll feel it later, I'm sure.

The door to Toby and Shiloh's room creaks open further to give the pup room to crawl out with his head hung low. It's obvious he's in the horrible state between drunk and hungover where your head is spinning, but your brain is coming back online.

Good.

I don't soften a damn thing, not my voice, not my glare, not my stance when he gives me his puppy dog eyes and whines.

"I don't give a flying fuck how much you had to drink last night. Why am I only finding out now that our new neighbor is your economics professor from last semester?"

Glancing around at the people who I trust most in the world, the feeling of betrayal inside of me is growing as I see the looks of guilt on Eli and Spencer's faces.

"And whose bright idea was it to make sure I know nothing about our new neighbor to the point that I wouldn't know I was picking him up at the club last night? Eli, Spencer? Any ideas on that one?"

The only sound that can be heard is the rhythmic sucking from Lucky with his binkie as I wait for someone to confess. Is it wrong that I still have hope that they didn't make the connection? Oh, God, please let them say they didn't realize...

Lucky gasps and his binkie falls from his mouth, making everyone turn to face him.

"Is Professor Barnes our new neighbor?!"

He's so innocent at times it hurts. I reach out to pull him into a hug while the tension in the room breaks with a few chuckles.

"Yes, Lucky," I tell him with a kiss to the top of his head. "Your Professor Barnes is the guy who moved into the back lot last week."

Raising my head to glare at the two Doms who knew,

I add, "And your Daddy and Uncle decided to not tell us who he is."

Lucky gasps again and turns on Spencer and Eli. I wouldn't have risked upsetting him if he was big, but little Lucky has no problem with feeling things. He's come a long way, actually. Stomping over to the other men, he punches Eli in the stomach and kicks his Daddy in the shin.

Everyone is taken aback by that. One thing our resident little is not is *violent*.

"You are both assholes of the highest order for this!" he yells at them, obviously no longer little. "If you ever fucking hide things from me again, I will... I will... I'll poop on your heads!"

Keeping my laughter silent has tears coming to my eyes. He was doing so well, too.

Spencer pulls his boy into his arms for a hug while Eli ruffles his nephew's curls. I know Lucky won't stay mad at them, but his outburst took a lot of my ire away. Very few people in my life have felt anger on my behalf, so when it happens, I really take the time to commit it to memory.

"As adorable as this all has been, why is the brat queen screaming at bird thirty?" Scott yawns, leaning back on Jace. "Do we all have to bear witness to you holding court, your majesty? Or can I go back to sleep? I have at least two more hours before I have to be awake and I gotta test four games today."

Doing my best to paste on an apologetic look, I give Scott and the others a nod that signals they don't have to be here if they didn't know. Jace and Scott both go back to their rooms, but Shiloh is clinging to Jay, who leads him downstairs with the promise of ice cream and video games.

Something pushing on my leg makes me look down to see Toby nudging me and looking up with tears in his eyes. A soft whine comes out of his throat, and I have to fight off my own tears. I know better than to be negative toward someone in subspace, or in his case pupspace, unless it has been properly negotiated with safewords and precautions.

"Go to bed, pup," I tell him softly as I run my fingers through his tangled hair. "We'll talk about this when you're back to being people. You're not a bad puppy, but you weren't a very good friend."

Toby pushes his nose against my palm before crawling back into his room. Pulling his door closed, I turn to look at the three people left. Spencer sighs and picks Lucky up in his arms. Heading for the stairs to the third floor, he tells us we should talk in the lounge up there.

"I didn't mean to keep it from you," Spencer says after putting Lucky to bed in their room. "I didn't want to say anything in case the name was just a coincidence."

I snort as I use their coffee maker to brew a cup. Lucky has excellent taste in coffee and creamers, so I take advantage of their stash any time I'm up here.

"Seriously, E," he says as he pulls another two mugs out of the cabinet. "I went to check him out last semester when I went to pick up Lucky from class, and I didn't see anyone who looked like the guy I remembered from when we were kids.

"Then, he was introduced to us as Matt when he moved in. He was one of Jackson's friends, so I didn't think anything of it. It wasn't until Toby recognized him at the club last night that I put it all together. I raced after you, but you were already running away."

The shame in Spencer's voice is undeniable, but turning to Eli, I know who I should really be angry with.

"And you?" I glare at him as I sip my glorious liquid ambrosia. "What do you have to say for yourself?"

The smaller man sighs and collapses onto the sofa with his head in his hands. When he looks up at us, there are tears in his eyes. I don't think I've ever seen Eli in so much pain as he's been these last few days, but I can't let it affect me. Holding on to my anger is a struggle, but I somehow manage.

"I knew who he was after the first time I met him," he confesses quietly. "Some of the stories he told with Jackson when we were drinking at Pegasus reminded me of some of the good stories you shared in the beginning about your childhood. I ran a background check on him, telling him it was for the rental.

"I didn't want to let him slip away if he really was your Mattie, not before you could find out what really happened. I know how those what if and why questions eat at a person, and I wanted to at least let you have closure."

"Then why didn't you *tell me*?" I hiss, slamming the coffee mug down on the counter. "You obviously knew it was him when you moved him in, so why did I have to play fucking Sherlock Holmes to figure it out *after* fucking him?!"

Tears start falling down my face at the betrayal. I can see how bad he feels, but my God! He *knew* my Mattie was less than a hundred yards away for all this time.

"You *know*. You BOTH know what Mattie has always meant to me. Why? Why would you do this to me?"

Eli speaks as Spencer pulls me against his chest.

"He doesn't seem to remember you at all. I didn't want you to get hurt, not this time of the year."

Pushing away from Spencer I look at both of them in shock. How did I not notice it before? They aren't any better than the asshole I escaped.

"What? Worried the little crazy boy is gonna off himself if his first crush doesn't recognize him? Is that it?" I relish the looks of pain on their faces. How *dare* they try to control me like this!?

"Well, I'll save you the trouble of your worry. I'm moving out today. I'll send someone for anything I forget."

"Eric, please," Spencer pleads and reaches for my arm. I jerk out of his reach and stare at his audacity to even attempt to touch me. "It was wrong to keep the secret, but you have to understand where Eli was coming from. We were planning on doing something in a couple weeks to get you guys introduced."

Inwardly, I wince at the harshness of my laughter, but I know I look like a cold hearted bitch. Sassy makes one hell of a mask when I am dying inside. I have perfected how to be a different person, hiding the screaming little boy inside.

"Fuck you both," I spit at them. "Don't even think of guilting me into staying somewhere I can't trust the people living with me. *You* did this. Remember that when the others ask where I am."

Managing to hold my anger until I reach my room, I break as soon as I open my door. I don't want to say goodbye. I don't want to leave Manor Drive. I know the intrusive thoughts will win if I leave, but they pushed me into this.

Happy Birthday to me.

18

MATT

I don't normally like to run for my exercise, but I need to move or else I'm going to wear a hole in the floor of my trailer pacing before my mother shows up for lunch. Throwing on a hoodie and sweats, I lace up my sneakers and head outside.

It's still early enough on a Sunday that hardly anyone is awake, especially in this neighborhood.

Jax told me almost everyone in the park works unconventional jobs or has non-traditional families.

I will do almost anything to escape the memories of how I failed both Eric and my new cutie.

I let my sneakers pound the pavement to drown out the memory of the day I signed a deal with the devil.

Fifteen Years Ago:

"You know you are smart enough for all of those fancy schools, Mattie," Mom says as she puts the garlic bread into the oven. "I know you love me, but spread your damn wings, already!"

I chuckle while I continue chopping vegetables for the salad. The Mendletons are having some sort of business dinner tonight and gave Mom barely three hours notice, so I'm helping out wherever I can. Unfortunately for me, this means that I am unable to escape the third degree about where I'm planning on applying for college.

"I'm still only a junior, Mom," I tell her as she passes by on the way to the stove to stir the sauce for the pasta. "I have plenty of time to make a decision."

I'm planning on sticking as close to home as possible for her. Ever since Dad passed away, I'm all that she's got left. My grandparents were all gone long before I was born, and neither Mom nor Dad had any siblings. I always wondered what it would be like to have a bigger family, but all things considered, I'm fine with it.

"Do I smell garlic bread?!" my favorite little dude squeals as he slides into the kitchen wearing what appears to be the tablecloth as a toga. Eric is the only son of Alan and Linda Mendleton, eleven years old and in desperate need of attention at all times.

My mom pulls him into a hug as he bites into the piece of the bread she handed him. I know if it were possible, she'd adopt him in a heartbeat. The Mendleton family is not exactly a loving one, and Eric deserves all of the love this world can offer. He has mood swings and acts out, but I'm pretty sure he can't help it. Mom wants him to be tested, but the last employee who suggested it was fired the next day.

"Lewis, my boy," Mr. Mendleton's voice echoes from the hallway. "Please come see me in my study while your mother finishes preparations for tonight's dinner."

I share a glance with Mom but leave my stool to follow the instructions. I might not be an actual employee here, but I know better than to make things more difficult for my mother. I can't fathom what Mr. Mendleton might want with me, but I'm not going to make him wait.

"Yes, sir?" I say from the doorway to his opulent study. I swear this man and his wife looked up every caricature of being wealthy and decided to outdo it.

He indicates that he would like me to take a seat at one of the godawful uncomfortable wingback chairs in front of his desk and I struggle to hide my disgust at the stale scent of cigar smoke that puffs out of the cushion when I sit.

"You graduate high school next year. Do I have that right, Lewis?" he asks as he pulls some documents out of the drawer to his right and sets them in front of me. NYU is my dream school. It is one hell of a school for economics, and I would love to immerse myself into the Big Apple.

"As an alumnus, I have some pull with the admissions board," the man in front of me says as he sits back in his chair. "I can not only get you in, but I will cover all four years of your degree plus room and board and a sizeable living allowance."

I have no doubt that if this were a cartoon, my jaw would be literally on the floor at this point with my eyes the size of dinner plates. Mr. Mendleton has never shown an ounce of interest in me, my studies, nor my future. Shaking myself out of it, I prepare for the catch.

"That is, of course, if you are able to meet my requirements. You will leave the day after your graduation and are not to return to this house ever again. You will not write, nor call, any person who lives here or else the costs of your education will be cut off."

My mind races through all of the possible reasons for why he could be asking this of me. Did I not do a good enough job of hiding my disdain for their way of life? Did I do something to piss off his wife again? His mistress?

"Your mother will of course be given a housing stipend for if she would prefer to live off property once you are gone," he adds with a wave of his hand. "I know she would quit if you could not come visit her, and we are far too old to break in a new servant."

When I come out of my memory, I realize I'm at the split in the road. I glance over toward the big manor house while I pause to catch my breath.

Movement by the garage draws my attention, and I see my cutie wiping his eyes as he lifts himself into the cab of a big ass truck.

I don't know who upset him, but I will destroy them.

I never asked if there was any rule against us going up to the house, but I don't really give a shit about it at this point. This beautiful man is sobbing and in pain in the cab of a truck. There isn't a universe where I wouldn't want to make him smile. One night, just a few hours, and he stole my heart.

He jumps and wipes hurriedly at his face when I knock on the hood of the truck. Giving a small smile, he rolls down the driver's side window and leans out.

"Hey hott stuff," he tries to be sultry but there's too much force behind it. "Want a ride back to your place?"

I open the driver's side door and make him slide over to the passenger side as I climb in. I have to resist the urge to pull him into my side, but instead I glance in the bed of the truck to see suitcases and bags.

"Did they kick you out or something?" I ask in confusion. "They don't seem like that kind of guys, but if they are then I'm going back to my mom's couch."

A watery giggle comes from my right and I see a real smile on his face.

He's beautiful.

"They..." He swallows a few times before he manages to steel himself to continue. "They didn't kick me out. I decided to leave..."

Something tells me there's more to the story, so I start the truck and pull out on the road directly into the trailer park. I don't give a fuck about the lawn, so I pull his truck directly onto the grass on my lot behind my trailer. If he wants to hide away from his roommates, he can hide right here.

"The landlord is going to make you pay for the landscaping if this gets stuck," he giggles out. I'm just glad that his sadness has passed for now. Judging by how quickly his mood shifted, yeah, Clarence was right. He's in a full blown manic phase.

"Alright, Cutie, Let's sneak inside and then you can tell me who I have to plan the demise of over some breakfast."

He shuffles up to my front door and lets himself in like he already lives there.

If I can convince him to say yes, he will by the end of the day.

Before heading inside, I reach into the bed of the truck and grab his big suitcase and a couple of the bags to bring into the house. Maybe he won't notice that I'm moving him in before asking. Setting his stuff down next to the futon, I don't see him in the immediate area. I can hear water running from the bathroom, so I leave him to it and go out to grab the rest of his things.

After I have all of his stuff in my living room, he still hasn't made an appearance. Glancing down the hallway, I notice my bedroom door is open. I should have figured he wouldn't be able to resist being a snoop. Chuckling to myself, I head into the kitchen to start making something to eat.

"You good with eggs, Cutie?" I call out but get no response.

Closing the fridge, I head down the hall to see what he's up to. Reaching my bedroom, I find the little minx asleep in the middle of my bed, clutching my pillow. Shaking my head, I turn to leave the room when I notice Eric's painting is missing from the wall above the bed.

Fear grips me, and I have to resist the urge to shake

the man in the bed until he wakes up so I can demand what the fuck he did with the only treasure I have from that beautiful boy.

Logic finally filters in and I realize it must have fallen behind the headboard while I was out running. Exhaling, I grab the blanket from the foot of the bed and go to tuck in my surprise houseguest. Leaning over him, I notice the painting lying on the bed between him and the wall.

Why the fuck would he want that on the bed with him?

"Mattie, don't leave me," he whimpers as I step into the hallway.

I freeze. I never told him I go by Matt, let alone Mattie.

"Please come back, Mattie," he mumbles in his sleep while I'm impersonating a statue in the doorway. "I didn't mean to make you leave. I'll be a good boy. You don't have to love me back..."

Before my brain can catch up to my body, I am outside, gulping in air like I've just run a mile. Eric is my cutie. Eric fucking Mendleton is the man who stole my heart last night.

No.

Eric stole my heart the very first time I met him. I just never realized my love would shift from brotherly to this all encompassing passion he lights inside of me now. Torn between joy and pure unadulterated shock, I start laughing.

By the time Clarence and Eli find me, I'm sitting on

the curb with tears streaming down my face trying to catch my breath again.

My unicorn escaped his evil father's clutches.

19

ERIC

Raised voices from outside wake me up. I didn't mean to fall asleep, but Mattie's bed is so freaking comfy. I bury my face in his pillow and take a deep breath. I love the way he smells. He doesn't use stinky aftershave and the Axe body spray craze definitely never crossed his path. Even as a kid, he always smelled like clean laundry and Mattie.

The blanket pools at my lap when I sit up. I don't remember grabbing the blanket...

My hand bumps something hard and I see the painting I pulled down from the wall. My lips twitch up in a smile against my will.

Eli said he forgot me. He didn't. He said he would keep this forever and he did.

"I don't give a flying fuck what you think is best, Eli!" Matt's raised voice brings me back to the present. "He isn't a child! You had no right to keep this to yourself!"

Creeping over to the window, I peek through the

curtains to see Matt arguing with Eli. Clarence is standing off to the side looking at Eli in shock. *I know the feeling oh frenemy of mine.* They've gone from yelling to speaking quietly. I hate that I can't listen in, but when I bump into the window crank handle, I smirk.

They'll never notice the window opening...

"I get it," Clare-issa explains it all says to Eli. *I doubt you get it Clare Bear, but go for it.*

"But you can't protect him from everything. Remember who it was that brought him to you. I know exactly what is at risk, probably better than you do. You didn't meet him until I had already been working with him for six months."

I rub at my temple hoping to get the drummer in my brain to knock it off so that I can hear what is said next, but Clarence the douche leads the other two men toward his place. Judging by the way Eli doesn't try to push into the trailer, I don't think he knows I'm here. He means well, but I'm still not happy at the fact that he's been acting like he's my keeper and I'm some poor creature at the zoo.

With my entertainment wandering off, the pounding in my head becomes more persistent. I only had one drink last night, so I shouldn't be hungover. Is it from the crying? Am I dehydrated?

Fuck. Did I take my pills this morning? Did I take them last night? Did I even eat yesterday?

Where are my pills? Did I pack them in my rush to leave the house? Are they in the truck?

SHIT!

They can't be in fluctuating temperatures and my bags have just been sitting in the bed of the truck for who the fuck knows how long. Please, oh please, don't let me have fucked my entire supply of my medications again. I don't want to go through withdrawals again waiting for a new prescription.

Racing to the front of the trailer, I jump off the steps and run to my truck only to discover the bed is empty. Did someone steal my shit?

Eli...

Did he take all my stuff back to the house? Is that fucking sadist going to hold me prisoner because I yelled at him?

My head feels like someone is repeatedly stabbing my left temple with a pencil and the counter strike is pounding behind my right ear. It hurts to even stand, so I sit down to lean against my back tire. The metal of the hubcap feels good against my throbbing temple, so I lean against it, hoping for enough relief to get up and find my pills.

I just need a minute for the drummer to take a break.

"Cutie? Why are you sleeping out here on the ground?"

I try to answer Mattie, but the only sound that comes out is a whimper, not me telling him I only need a minute. Moving my head hurts like a bitch. His arms wrap around my back and under my legs and suddenly I'm airborne. I can't stop the cry of pain when I open my eyes and the light stabs through them.

"It's alright sweet boy," Mattie murmurs softly as I

hear the door close behind us. "Is it a headache or something more?"

I can't seem to talk, but I manage to somehow indicate it's my head that is the problem because Matt lays me down on something soft and moments later, there is a cool rag laying on my forehead.

"Is this a migraine?" his voice asks as the room beyond my eyelids gets darker. "Or is something wrong? Do we need to go to the hospital?"

I shake my head and whimper as the spikes drive further into my brain.

"Pills" I manage to push the word out. I am not even sure if he heard me until I hear the sounds of zippers and rustling. I really hope he's not just trying to get me some ibuprofen. Then again, it might cut through enough that I can find out what Eli did with my stuff.

"Found it, I think," he says from a lot closer than he was before. I open my eyes into the darkened room and see my Mattie kneeling next to the sofa, no the futon. He has a futon because he is probably just like Jackson and spends money on the dumbest things and not on the important things like fashion and décor. He is holding up something in his hand and I have to squint to make out that it's my pill case. My headache is making me see double.

I give him a thumbs up as he helps me sit up and dumps the pills into my hand. I toss them back dry before I notice the bottle of water he just opened for me. Snickering at me, he holds the bottle to my lips while I drink down some water to chase the medications.

Hydration won't hurt with how much I was crying earlier.

After helping me lay back down, Matt gives me a kiss on the cheek with a promise we will talk after he comes back from lunch with his mother. He hasn't called me by my name yet. I just hope I can get him to fall in love with me as a man instead of as his adorable little brother.

"Get some rest," he whispers from the doorway. "Your phone is in the kitchen charging. My number is on the fridge if you need me before I get back."

I'm certain it's my imagination after the door closes. There's no way he said he loves me already. Closing my eyes, I let the cool towel and darkness sweep me into dreamland.

20

MATT

Twenty minutes after giving my boy a goodnight kiss for his nap, I walk in the front door of my mother's house.

It would have been five minutes less had Eli not stopped me on the way out. He felt the need to apologize to me again, but like I told him at least five times before that. He owes that apology to Eric.

He isn't a burden. He isn't someone to manage. His disorder needs managed, but the man needs to be loved and respected.

Setting my keys on the kitchen counter, I'm surprised to see Mom sitting at the kitchen table clutching a cup of coffee like it holds the secrets of the universe. She smiles at me when I come in the room, but her face returns to looking troubled as I pour myself a cup and join her.

"I'm sorry I had to change it up to having lunch here," I tell her as I sit down. "A friend needed to escape his roommates for the day, and I offered up my place before I remembered about our lunch."

Honestly, I would have loved to surprise both of them with lunch, but since Eric is suffering from the withdrawal headaches from his medication, I'm not going to pressure either of them to have a reunion today.

"I have to tell you something, Mattie," Mom says, reaching across the table to grab my hand in hers. The tone of her voice and the way she is acting...

No!

It can't be!

"Don't tell me the cancer is back," I grab her hand in both of mine.

I can't lose her.

My mother is the only family I have. I won't survive it.

The only reason I was able to stay strong the first time was that I had Sylvia to give me hope of a future, even though she never bothered to come to visit.

Mom pats my hands with her free one and gives me a soft smile. "No, Mattie, it's not the cancer. I'm still in remission and the doc says there's a good chance it will stay that way. The surgery was a success after all. This has to do with the reason I quit working for the Mendletons. I never told you my reasons because I didn't want you to risk your career or your relationship with Sylvia."

I can't possibly imagine anything so world ending aside from losing my mother that would cause me to be irrational enough to destroy my life over. Especially now that I know Eric got away from his father unscathed.

If it wasn't for the fact that Mom looks so torn up, I

would think the only information I care about would be if that asshole died.

"Do you remember the story in the news about the hockey team about five years ago?" she asks and my brain short circuits. Okay, so that came out of left field. That definitely isn't where I was expecting this to go, but I nod.

Five years ago there was a huge scandal at one of the local colleges when their hockey team gang raped a girl. The school went from being one of the top schools in the country to essentially being blacklisted. They lost all of their funding for athletics and a lot of alumni were put under the microscope for years.

"They never released the victim's name," she continues. "Unfortunately, that case was linked to the recent murder for hire case that made national news a few months ago. It wasn't supposed to happen, but somehow the press leaked the identity of the original victim yesterday to national outlets."

I sip at my coffee wondering if I knew the girl at all. The age group would mean she would have been at least half a decade younger than I am.

Maybe she was someone's little sister?

"Mattie hon, I don't want you flying off the handle, baby," she says and I give her a reassuring smile. I've never had much of a temper in the first place, but Mom is a worrier. She passes over her tablet so that I can read the trending story.

DRAG ME UP

From Captain·to·Convict:
Appeals Board Overturns Sentencing

After six weeks of grueling testimony and insurmountable evidence, Tibalt University Hockey Captain Rafe Dennison was found guilty of all charges related to the incident at the home of former teammate and alumnus Andrew Streaker almost five years ago.

The turning point in the trial was not testimony of the victim or other witnesses from the party even though the victim recounted vivid details that coincided with the lab results from the hospital. However, the nail in Mr. Dennison's proverbial coffin was the testimony of his former teammate, Donald Hastings, regarding the fact that several members of the team had taken money to drug the victim for a blackmail scheme and then decided to assault him on their own.

Mr. Hastings has plead guilty to conspiracy and has received his sentence of six months of probation as a result.

For the crimes he had been convicted of, Mr. Dennison was sentenced to up to ten years in prison without the possibility of parole. In light of the testimony provided during the recent case of The State of Pennsylvania v. Sabrina Carlisle, the appeals board overturned the decision of denying parole.

Mr. Dennison's attorney had this to say, "With Mr. Mendleton and Mr. Hastings both admitting to the coercions and manipulations of Ms. Carlisle as the impetus for the crime, we believe the courts justly under-stood that Mr. Dennison has served enough time for an unfortunate drunken encounter. He maintains to this day that he had no knowledge that Mr. Mendleton had not given consent."

The parole hearing for Mr. Dennison is scheduled to take place within the month. With all of the evidence provided in the Carlisle trial, experts

agree that parole will likely be granted as long as Mr. Dennison has no
disciplinary issues during his incarceration.

Mr. Mendleton? MR. MENDLETON?!

My world implodes as the memories of what I know of that time assault me. News articles on the headline pages of the search engines that I clicked away from. Changing the channel every time the national news tried to talk about anything dealing with the trial. I was disgusted by it and embarrassed that it happened in my hometown. I was even more disgusted at the fact that I went to school with the piece of shit that owned the house. I looked up to Streaker when I was a teenager and yet he provided the environment where this could happen to someone.

It wasn't some random girl. It was Eric. *My* Eric was drugged and raped and dragged through the repeated abuse that the legal system puts victims through. And now the world knows it was him.

"I have to go to him," I say as I jump up from the table, spilling my coffee onto the floor. But my mom grabs my hand to pull me into a hug. I'm shaking from the anger and guilt and shame but the woman who is my world just holds me together.

"His father threw him out five years ago," she whispers as she holds me tight. "I never knew the reason but as soon as that boy was free, I quit."

Mom leads me to the sofa and pulls me down next to her. I knew she quit five years ago, but I never asked why.

I only figured she had saved enough for retirement. I never realized she stayed only for Eric.

"I don't know where he went to or what has happened to him since he left that house, but I know he is alive. He sends me a card every Christmas and birthday, but never includes a return address. I don't even know where you could even go to look for him."

"He'll be alright, Mom," I tell her, hoping that I didn't just lie to her face. If anything happens to Eric because of this media fuckup, I will burn them all.

21

MATT

"Mattie, do you know that Spencer boy's number? He might know where Eric is."

Pulling Mom into a hug, I thank the universe for bringing him to me before I knew all of this. I know for a fact that if I knew about this before last night, we never would have happened. He would have remained my little boy to protect and not become the man I love.

"I will give Spencer a call," I promise her while she berates me for a few more minutes about all of the ways I can find her little boy to make sure he is alright. I was planning on telling her how we met, minus the sexy bits, but today is not going to be the day.

While Mom is making some grilled cheese sandwiches and tomato soup for lunch, I pull up my security camera feed for my living room. I have a pinhole camera on my TV since it's the most valuable thing I own, but it also gives a good room view as an extra precaution. Eric is still sleeping on the futon, so I exit the app and send a text to Spencer. I'm still pissed at Eli, but the guys need to be aware.

> **LMB:**
> Have you checked the news today?

> **Spencer:**
> I try not to get depressed. Y?

> **LMB:**
> Does the name Rafe Dennison ring a bell?

My phone starts ringing before I can even continue. I swipe across the screen to answer and head for the front porch.

"I gotta take a phone call, Ma!" I call out before I close the door behind me.

"News better be an obit for that piece of shit," Spencer growls out as I sit on the swing my mother put on her small porch.

"Parole hearing next month," I tell him. There's no reason to beat around the bush on this. It's obvious Spencer knows about it by his recognition of the name.

"Bastard was sentenced without the possibility of parole. What the fuck?!"

"Something about Eric's testimony in a trial recently got him the appeal."

"Fuck!" he shouts as the sound of glass breaking comes across the line.

I just sit and listen to his breathing until he gasps.

"Daddy?"

The voice in the background is vaguely familiar, but one thing is for certain and that is the fear behind it.

"Shit. Matt, I'm gonna have to call you back," he says as he is attempting to calm the other person who is crying loudly in the background. "Or better yet, I'll swing by."

"I'll text you when I'm back home. I'm at my mom's for lunch. She showed me the news article."

"Got it, yeah. That will work," he says and I'm ready to hang up when he speaks again.

"Wait, how did you know this is dealing with Eric? Did he tell you about it?"

The crying on the other side of the phone stops and I hear a little voice ask, "Did someone hurt my Princess Eric? I'll beat them up." There's what sounds like a kid impersonating a wolf followed by a giggle.

"The article named Mr. Mendleton as the victim, and I'm pretty damn sure it wasn't talking about his piece of shit father."

"Fuck," Spencer whispers something to whoever he is with and then adds to me, "Hope you don't mind company. We are going to need to have a house meeting, but I doubt Eric will want to come back home yet. Is an hour long enough to have lunch and get home?"

I hate the thought of cutting and running on my mom, but if I tell her it's for Eric she will shove me out the door. Actually, that isn't a bad idea. I don't want to spring everyone on him in addition to the news. I tell Spencer that unless he hears differently from me, an hour is fine. I want to make sure that Eric has recovered from his headache and I can prepare him for the news.

"Mom?" I call out as head to the kitchen for my keys. I grab them and kiss her on the cheek. "That was Spencer and we are going to meet up with Eric to see how we can help."

She doesn't say anything, but hands me a couple containers holding soup and sandwiches. Leaning down, I let her give me a kiss on my cheek.

"Go take care of our little boy, Mattie."

22

ERIC

The feeling of lips brushing against my forehead doesn't fit with the wonderful memory I'm reliving in my dream. Mattie took me for hot chocolate and he kept getting whipped cream all over his face to make me laugh. He went to so many lengths to make me smile when I was a kid.

"Sorry, kiddo. No whipped cream in the house but I do have a cupcake for you."

My eyes shoot open in surprise and for a second I'm confused on where the fuck I am. The soft chuckle coming from my left lets the fear subside. Turning over, I lock eyes with Matt who is crouching next to the futon, petting my head softly.

"Hi," I greet him with a shy smile. "I thought I dreamed you up."

"You're the one who has always been magic, my unicorn boy," he tells me and my heart stutters.

HE KNOWS IT'S ME!

I launch myself off the futon and tackle him to the floor in a hug. Planting my lips on his, I fully intend to show him how much I have missed him, but he pushes me up so that I'm straddling him on the floor.

"I can work with this, but can I get some padding for my knees?" I ask with a saucy wiggle of my eyebrows. Mattie just chuckles in response, so I stand and help him to his feet.

"Just saying, I can work with whatever," I tell him and get a smack to my ass for my trouble.

Oh, Daddy...

Wait a second. I don't want a Daddy, do I? I'm not little.

"Happy Birthday, Eric," he says as he pulls me to his chest. "I'm so sorry I've missed so many of them."

I don't know if I want to feel happy or sad at that. I'd like to think that over the years, I became numb to not having anyone celebrate my birthday. It's not like my parents ever cared when I was growing up. Hell, the only times I've ever had any type of celebration for me was from Ms. Sara and Matt and the rest of the staff when my parents were away on my birthday. If they were home, there would be a grown up party, but nothing for *me*.

"We have to have a kind of serious discussion, Cutie," Matt says as he pulls back from our hug. "Serious talk now, sexy talk later."

He knows me so well.

"The guys from the house want to come over for a meeting to discuss something that came up today. I have my tablet on the coffee table there. Read the article I pulled up while I get our lunch together. We'll talk about it after we eat and come up with a plan with the rest of the guys if that's alright with you."

Turning back to the coffee table, I pick up the tablet. Hitting the button to wake it up, I realize Matt doesn't have any kind of security on it.

"If you're still up for it after the meeting, we're going to celebrate your birthday. We can ask them to stay for it, or it can be just the two of us. It's your call."

"You shouldn't be so trusting with your devices," I mumble, but I'm secretly happy that he trusts me with it. "If I want them to stay, I'll ask you for birthday kisses. If I don't, I'll grab myself a Sprite. You do have Sprite, don't you?"

He chuckles and grabs me a can of my favorite beverage out of the fridge before I start reading.

"The store didn't have the good root beer. I still don't understand how you can drink that stuff," he says as he hands me the can of lemon-lime pop.

"I don't drink root beer anymore," I mumble. All teasing thoughts flee from my brain as I read. My brain doesn't want to process what it's seeing. I was supposed to remain anonymous. Father paid off *everyone*. He tried to kill me because he had to spend more money to keep his name out of it than if he just had to pay them off to not report it.

"He's going to kill me," I say under my breath. I guess Matt has good hearing because a second later, I'm in his arms. One of the sandwiches fell off the plate and soup has sloshed all over his coffee table.

"You need to be more careful with your furniture," I tell him as I wiggle out of his arms to reach for a sandwich. "Even if it is cheaper than a hooker down on Liberty."

I got no issue with sex workers, but there's a difference between pricing to the market and selling yourself short. Those ladies and gents don't know their worth, and I've helped a few move on to better and safer places to find their johns. The ones heading to Liberty are there for the spectacle, not to make a transaction.

If I pretend what I just read doesn't exist, it goes away, right? The monster in my nightmares isn't going to be free. My sperm donor isn't going to hunt me down to kill me. The world hasn't just been told I was gang raped.

"Eric, are you okay with the guys coming over for the meeting?"

I shrug and watch as Matt gets up to grab a roll of paper towels to clean up his mess. After he mops up the spilled soup, he pulls out his phone but keeps glancing at me instead of doing anything on it. He looks conflicted.

I keep chewing my sandwich. It was nice of Ms. Sara to give Matt food to bring back for me. I know what it *should* taste like, but it tastes like ash. Actually, no it doesn't. It tastes like nothing.

"Why do people say something tastes like ash when they mean it tastes like nothing? Ash tastes disgusting. I know. I've tried it."

Matt stops wiping up the soup and looks at me like I'm an alien. Can I really pull off not being affected?

Apparently, I've shut down too much. I need to do something to get his mind off of worrying about me.

Something settles inside of me as an idea forms: If I keep him distracted, I can delay talking about it. Distracting, I can do. I'm a master at keeping a man's attention where I want it.

I practically inhale the rest of my sandwich to have my hands free for my plan. Cuddling back into his arms I let my hands move over his chest, dipping lower and lower. I have more than enough experience to know how to turn a man on, and I can tell Matt is enjoying my attention.

"What are you doing, Eric?" he gasps out as I flip open the button on his jeans. I mean, I would think it's pretty obvious, but I give him a signature Sassy smirk as I reach under the waistband of his delightfully boring boxer briefs to grasp his hard cock in my hand. Slowly stroking him, I stretch up to give my Mattie a kiss on the cheek.

"I'd think it's obvious, lover," I tell him with as sultry a voice as I can manage with the panic running rampant inside my head. "I'm looking for attention. A very specific type of attention if you get my drift."

Matt's hips lift off the futon as he tries to hold off his orgasm and regain control of the situation, but I've got him in the palm of my hand, quite literally. Unlike last night, I'm the one in control of this encounter.

"Eric... Cutie... Please... Can't..."

Matt is fighting his need to come, but I can tell he wants to. Not only is he smiling at me, but he could easily reach down and grab my hand to stop me. Instead, he is clutching the back of the futon frame for dear life. His breathing is erratic. His weak protests have turned into moans as he thrusts into my hand now, his precum serving as an adequate enough lubricant.

I guess my Mattie likes a little pain with his pleasure. We can take advantage of this later on at the club.

Matt's entire body tenses, and I watch the ecstasy flow across his face. The sound of his groan reverberates through me to the point I just want to drag him back to the bedroom so we can have our wicked way with each other for the rest of the day. Hell, the rest of eternity. I try to stand up, but his hand reaches out for my wrist to pull me back to his side.

Eh, the futon works, too. It's not like we have to worry about roommates or anything.

Before I am able to kiss him, there is a knock on the back door. I'm fully prepared to ignore it, but Mattie groans in frustration and tells whoever it is that the door is open. I *want* to go back to making him groan for another reason and tell the person at the door to fuck off. Instead, I hurriedly grab some tissues to clean off my hand while Matt tucks himself back into his jeans.

23

MATT

"You're early," I snarl at Spencer when he walks into my living room. Eric is sitting next to me, wiping my release off his hand with the tissues as if it's nothing to be concerned about. The sight makes my dick start to wake back up. Hell, who am I kidding? I'm still hard to the point where this meeting is going to be extremely uncomfortable.

"My boy was anxious to make sure his best buddy was alright," Spencer tells us as I notice a head of chocolate colored curls poke in the doorway. It's been a few months, but I recognize Lucas from last semester.

"Lucas is your boy?"

The man in question shuffles into the room like a kid who got caught sneaking out for a snack after bedtime. Toe-ing the floor with his colorful canvas high tops, he glances at me through his curls to give a small smile.

"Hi, Professor Barnes," he says shyly. "Are you going to be Eric's Daddy? He needs a Daddy. I don't mind loaning out Spencer, but he deserves one of his own and I want my Daddy to have more Daddy friends."

I'm sure my face is doing a pretty fair imitation of a goldfish at this point. I mean, Eli and Jackson told me the house was nicknamed Kink Manor, and Clarence works at a BDSM club. But I never really let those facts sink in for what it meant for their relationships and those that live in the house.

Eric collapses into my side with laughter. Spencer is coughing in an attempt to cover his own mirth. Lucas looks confused, glancing between all of us. When his bottom lip starts to tremble, the laughter cuts off abruptly, and the two other men in my living room converge on him to reassure him.

"It's alright, Little One," Spencer says as he pulls the smaller man into his arms, lifting him onto his hip like he's carrying a child. "We aren't laughing at you. Matt just looks really funny with his fishy impersonation."

Eric nods emphatically and runs the hand that had not been down my pants through Lucas's curls. "Your professor isn't my Daddy. He's my Mattie. To me, that's so much better than some random Daddy."

"Daddy isn't random," the smaller man pouts. "He's my super special Daddy made just for me."

"You're right, Lucky," Eric says before giving a kiss to the forehead of his friend. "Spencer is a very special person... for a lot of people."

The look between my cutie and Spencer speaks of some secret. I don't know what happened there, but whatever holds these two men together is a bond forged in adamantium or some other unbreakable material.

"The others are on the way over," Spencer tells us as he sits on the other end of the futon, Lucas in his lap. "But I wanted to give you a bit more of a crash course in everyone since we'll probably have a bit of regression and falling into safety spaces with this meeting."

Eric washes his hands in my kitchen sink and comes back to sit on my lap. It feels nice to have someone there. Grabbing another sandwich from the abandoned pile on my coffee table, he waves to indicate that he expects his friend will continue speaking.

"Thanks for the blessing, your majesty," he chuckles while the man on his lap giggles around the thumb now in his mouth. I'm so confused.

"How much do you know about BDSM, specifically the softer sides and dynamics?"

I hold up my hand in the pinching gesture. I know what I've read in my mother's romance books, but not enough to truly understand it. Spencer spends the next twenty minutes giving me a crash course on kink and dynamics, including how it manifests with everyone from the house.

By the time my rudimentary kink education is complete, my living room is packed with all the guys from the house plus my new neighbors Ash, Clarence, Theo, Steve, and Avery – who works as a reporter for a local news station.

"Has everyone read the article?" Eli asks the room. Every head nods while my boy tenses in my lap. I'm sure he is in fact *my* bratty boy at this point. I might actually be a Daddy by nature, but I like how Eric put it. I'm his Mattie.

Avery shifts on the stool she perched herself on at my breakfast bar. "The quote was supposed to redact Eric's name," she tells us. "The Mendleton's attorney has been cracking out cease and desist notices since it went to print this morning, but there's nothing to be done now that the name is out. It's a nightmare for the district attorney's office as well for allowing a victim's name to become public record."

Lucky, as I've come to discover Lucas prefers to be called, pops his thumb out of his mouth to say, "I hope the meanie from the trial lost his job for that. He didn't have to be such a ... such a... DOODY HEAD!"

It was hard not to at least smile at the outrage from the little, although I'm a bit lost as to what they're talking about.

"Are you talking about the Carlisle trial mentioned in the article?"

Lucky nods hard enough he almost tumbles off Spencer's lap, but Spencer is the one to answer.

"Eric was called to testify to prove that Sabrina had made a habit of her little scheme. Lucky wasn't her first target in the college sector. Eric was the first that they could actually trace to her. But..."

"But the asshats she bribed to target me didn't follow her rules, so she moved on to easier targets for a couple years before trying the college thing again with Lucky."

Eric interrupts whatever Spencer had been about to

say, and the man next to me looks relieved he didn't have to say whatever he was going to say.

"But what do we do about this?" Jay yawns from his perch on the floor under the window. "We don't need the press showing up at the house or Mister Drag to harass him further. There's already so much hate in the comments from those dumbass people victim blaming."

"I'll take care of that," Scott mumbles from his place next to where Jace sits with a very well loved teddy bear in his lap. "I've called in some favors to take care of monitoring the comments and tracking the most vitriolic ones to determine if additional steps need to be taken."

Spencer and Jay both roll their eyes with exaggerated sighs, but Eli looks hungry at that idea. Some others snicker, but almost everyone in the room is smiling... some looking downright sinister.

"What am I missing?" I ask Eric in a whisper.

Leaning back to whisper back in my ear, he tells me, "Scott is a genius with computers. He's a professional video game beta tester, but he claims he used to be part of some hacker network or something. He doesn't do it anymore, or so he says, but his connections have reportedly forced a few early retirements if you know what I'm saying."

I feel my eyebrows go up and look at the unassuming man. He's the consummate geek. His outfit consists of ripped jeans, basic canvas shoes, a hoodie with some video game reference that I don't understand. His messy short blond hair and huge black plastic rimmed glasses make him look like ninety percent of the computer engineering students I see on campus every day. Somehow, I thought assuming he worked with computers would be stereotyping.

"As nice as that is, Scotty, I think we need to focus on the immediate problem," Jackson pipes up as he grabs another beer from my fridge. When the fuck did he get here? "We need to make sure the vultures can't come after Eric or any of us. We might have to cancel our trip to DC this week."

A chorus of groans can be heard from half the room, but Eric waves at them to stop.

"That won't be necessary," he tells us all when the room quiets. "The only Mr. Mendleton in the city is my father and unless he tells the press what he forced on me when he kicked me out, they won't be able to find me. Thursday at the Devil won't be affected."

24

ERIC

The looks I get from around the room make me squirm. I love the spotlight, but this is like being a bug under a microscope.

"Explain," Eli commands from his spot, arms crossed in front of him. I stiffen at the order and struggle with the urge to go against it just for fuck's sake. You would never know this is the guy who has spent the last four years cleaning me up when I crash after my lack of inhibitions fucks up my life.

"Watch your tone," Matt snarls from behind me. "You aren't his Master. He isn't yours. He's mine. No one gets to speak to my boy that way."

Oh, hot damn. That was sexy as fuck! I'm really regretting not taking the time to replace the panties I forgot in the hotel room last night. These pants really don't do a good job hiding the way my dick is responding to this assertive side of my Mattie.

In the silence that follows, Matt gently asks me to

explain to everyone what I meant since we all need to be on the same page. It's like he is fine tuned into my brain and what triggers the stubborn defiance. I'm practically putty in his hands... I don't hate it.

Turning to the rest of the room, I take a deep breath and dive into the details of things I should have shared a long time ago.

"So, some of you know what happened to me five years ago in general terms," I say before I glance at Spencer and then over to Steve. "Some of you know a bit more detail, but I have never told anyone every detail of what happened, especially after."

"I don't want to know the details," Shiloh interrupts. "Can we skip to the after part? Or I can go back home. You don't need me here for this."

Before our kitten can get up to leave, Lucky jumps off Spencer's lap to hug him. "Eric can skip to the end. Or I'll hold my hands over your ears for the scary parts. You're family and this is a family meeting."

Nodding my head, I tell the room, "I'm not ready to share the full story with everyone just yet. But the end is something you all need to be aware of.

"So you all know how my father has always been obsessed with the image of the perfect family more than actually putting in any work to be a real family, right?"

Everyone in the room makes some indication of agreement. I chuckle at Matt and Spencer both snorting. Eli makes some sort of comment under his breath. I think I can make out the word "understatement" some- where in there.

"So when...*the event*... happened, my father tried to force me to drop the charges because of the negative light it was shining on our family name within the police force and the district attorney's office. The chief of police was his golfing buddy at the time."

The only ones in the room not surprised by this are Spencer, Clarence, and Eli. They were the ones who helped to pick me up after all. Closing my eyes, I fall back into my memory and tell my friends about the night my father tried to kill me for being a victim who was unwilling to let my abuser go free.

"You will tell the university that you were mistaken and you will rescind the police report!"

My father is still yelling at me to drop the charges against the hockey players that assaulted me. I can't stop the maniacal laughter that bubbles out in response. This is what finally breaks me. I can't keep doing this dutiful son routine with such a bastard.

"Your son was fucking attacked and you care more about the potential future careers of his fucking rapists than his own wellbeing!"

The look on his face is comical. I've never even talked back to my father, let alone raised my voice to him. But this... this event is the straw that fucking buries the camel.

"I never asked for your love," I continue while he's still impersonating a goldfish. "I never asked for your money. Hell, I never fucking asked to be born! You and whatever coochie I crawled out of didn't give me a fucking choice on anything.

"All I ever received from you in my twenty one years on this earth were shame, guilt, and abandonment issues. If you tell me one more time to drop the charges, I will make sure no one in this city, in this fucking country, will do business with you, you homophobic piece of shit."

I watch as my father's face morphs from shock to rage. There is nothing more he can do to hurt me. He can't touch my trust fund, and that will be mine unrestricted in just a few years. I can live with that

"You are no son of mine. Not anymore!" he screams at me and hauls me up out of the chair by my arm. He drags me from his study and throws me toward the stairs. I barely catch myself on the banister and turn back to look at him in shock.

I honestly didn't think he could do or say anything to hurt me any worse than I was already feeling.

I was wrong.

His hatred of my sexuality was one thing. This is a whole universe of hate. My father would rather kill me than face the scandal of having a gay son who was raped.

My father tried to kill me.

I run from my father's house without bothering to grab anything. All I know is I'm running for my life at this point. I saw my death in his eyes, the same eyes I see in the mirror every day.

I don't know how long I run, but I finally collapse on the steps of what looks like a club of some sort, miles away from home.

That is not my home anymore. I have no home. No one

wants me. Everyone abandons me eventually. I'm used goods. I'm broken. I've always been...

"Sugar, you okay?"

I look up into the gentlest eyes I've ever seen outside of Ms. Sara, Mattie's mom. The lady in front of me makes me feel the same way, like she's a real mom... not like the monster I was given to. Something inside of me that was barely there snaps, and I surrender to the heartache and emptiness that is now my life.

"That's the day I met Cleo for the first time," I tell the room as I open my eyes. "Clarence helped me get the small amount of stuff I had from my dorm and moved me onto his couch until a room opened up in Kink Manor.

"It took a while for my father's attorney to track me down, but he finally did after my deposition for the trial. They started the process for a legal name change for me. I had to choose a new name because I was no longer his son as far as he was concerned. I was told in no uncertain terms was I to contact him, and I was fine with that."

Matt pulls me back against his chest and squeezes me tight. "Is that why the hotel staff called you Mr. Pierce?"

I nod and look out at everyone in the room. "I refused to give up my first name, but agreed to change my surname. Pierce was originally my middle name. I legally completed the name change about six months ago. I forced him to wait so that I wouldn't have to jump through hoops when my trust fund was set to release on my twenty fifth birthday. Because I refused to change my name in the beginning, he paid out a rather exorbitant amount to make sure my name was buried and redacted in the original trial documents."

Everyone in the room is staring at me with varying levels of shock, except Matt.

"How didn't I know about this name change? I'm your boss," Clarence asks from his perch on Theo's lap.

"I made the change myself in my file and on the payroll roster. Call me paranoid, but I figured the less people knew about it, the safer I would be. You only have us listed by first name, so you never noticed it," I tell him. I only feel a little bit guilty. Mostly, I'm enjoying the look of annoyed outrage on his face. "You really should learn to be more creative with your password. Theo's birthday is not a secret among us."

The laughter that flows through the room is still tense until Lucky jumps up from petting Shiloh's back and exclaims, "You're like a secret agent! Daddy, he's a super spy!"

25

ERIC

Sipping on my Sprite, I watch as Mattie locks the door. After going through the details of my name change and the fact that my father is going to be on the warpath, we all came up with the plan that extra security cameras will be set up at McKinley's, the bar at the bottom of the hill, so that we can track all the vehicles coming up to our neighborhood. Clarence has already arranged for Theo to be at Mister Drag full time until this all blows over, letting someone else take over at the Devil for the next month for the front desk and security.

"I'm so sorry this happened on your birthday, Cutie."

I snuggle into his side when he sits down next to me on the futon. "It's not the worst thing to happen. Hell, it feels nice to be happy and loved on my birthday for a change. I haven't really had that since you left."

Matt stops his soft caress of the back of my neck and I can feel him tense. "Why did you leave like that?" I ask him tentatively. I've always been afraid of this answer. "Didn't you miss m... your mom?"

I barely manage to hold back the selfish question. Of course, he didn't miss the annoying brat who kept popping up. He was a teenager headed to college. What kid in college is thinking about the twelve year old son of his mother's boss?

"I missed you and your tablecloth dresses every day, my unicorn boy," he says as he kisses the top of my head. "I regretted the deal I made with your father almost immediately, but I didn't realize the ramifications and the fine print until that last day we saw each other."

I had to think back to the last time I saw him. I remember the day he left for college like it was yesterday. That was the worst day of my life, outside of *the event*. He wasn't at my graduation party, even though Spencer swears he saw him.

"The fountain?" I ask and he nods. That whole day was a blur. It was my sixteenth birthday and I had a bit of a concussion from flipping my brand new convertible. Father was so angry that day. That was when he took me to his doctors and I got put on so many mood stabilizers that I became a zombie.

"Father said you were disgusted with me and I had to stop being a child if I wanted to be respected as a man. I thought I dreamed you up that day as a manifestation of my happier past. You leaving was like the proof I needed to accept that my life was going to be shit and I needed to grow up"

I hear a sniffle from above me and see tears streaking down Matt's cheeks.

"Why did you leave me, Mattie?" I need to know the answer before we move further into this relationship. I didn't think of it before, but the conversation earlier made me realize that he could just walk away from me again. I can't do this with him if there's a chance of that happening again.

"I didn't know exactly why your father brought it up, but he offered to pay for my undergraduate degree at NYU as long as I didn't come home at all during those four years. I was seventeen and facing a mountain of debt to even go to community college, and he offered to pay for it all at my dream school: tuition, room and board, books, even an allowance."

As a kid, I would have never understood how this would be enough to get him to leave me. I worshipped the ground my Mattie walked on and would do anything to stay by his side. If he had explained back then, I wouldn't have understood. Hell, I probably would have found a way to stow away in his car like I did that Christmas.

But as an adult looking back, I get it. My parents paid their staff the bare minimum that they could get away with. Ms. Sara would have never been able to afford to help Mattie with college expenses. This deal with my father was a once in a lifetime opportunity for him.

"I can understand why you'd take that deal," I tell him honestly. "And I understand why you didn't try to explain when you left. I wouldn't have understood it back then. But why did you stay away?"

26

MATT

Oh, man.

I didn't expect to have to explain all of this right away. I kind of wanted to bask in that new relationship glow for a few days before we got into the deep stuff, but I guess we need to get the past behind us to move forward.

"I came home as soon as I graduated with my bachelor's degree," I tell him. "That was the day you wrecked your car into the fountain. After that, I was nicely informed that I was not allowed to contact you or come onto the property at all without being invited by your father unless I would have to repay everything he spent on my education."

My mind drifts back to that day as Eric contemplates exactly what I've told him.

Ten Years Ago:

Grabbing my aching head in my hand, I move across the gravel lot behind the garage toward the kitchen in the main house to find Mom. She left me a note to tell me where to find her, next to some ibuprofen and a bottle of water. The note was a brief scolding for making so much noise, but I know I'll get worse as soon as she has the opportunity to slam some pots and pans around.

"It's not a big deal!" a boy's voice is coming from around the corner of the main house, from the direction of the circular driveway out front. "I'm not a child anymore!"

"You are sixteen, Eric! You are most definitely a child, and apparently you cannot be trusted with a car if you managed to destroy this one just days after you received it!"

THAT voice I recognize. Mr. Mendleton is the absolute last person I want to see on this trip home. Yes, the family that employs my mother paid for my undergraduate education at a top tier university in New York City. Yes, they provided me with opportunities that I could never dream of, especially coming out of it debt free and being able to secure funding and scholarships for my graduate studies at the same university starting in the fall.

But this man hates me for some reason. All I've ever done is ensure his son didn't die of loneliness as a child. Apparently, this is the same son who at sixteen somehow destroyed his car. Knowing the asshat, it's probably a scratch or dent and the fucker is screaming at that precious boy for no reason.

My righteous outrage over the way the jackass is

berating my little unicorn buddy makes me alter my course to head for the front of the house to see the damage myself.

Is it the hangover or is my brain just not computing?

As soon as I round the corner, I can't make sense of what I'm seeing. There is a lime green convertible upside down on the fountain, causing water to spray across the driveway, cascading down toward the street. Even turning my head every possible way, I can't figure out how the fuck the car could even get there like that.

Mr. Mendleton notices me and storms inside yelling about how his son is lucky that this happened out of the eyes of the media. Welp, it sounds like the asshole still loves his image more than his own flesh and blood.

I should probably turn the water off to the fountain. Turning toward the garage, I try to remember where the shutoff for the fountain is located. I think it's on the same wall as the solar panels backup battery for the gate.

A soft gasp has me turning back toward the house. When I see the young man sitting on the stairs, it takes me too long to equate him to the gangly twelve year old I left behind four years ago. Before I can even say anything, he launches himself into the air and I have no choice but to catch him.

I promised a long time ago to never let him fall. I don't mean to ever let him go again. These four years were torture, hearing Mom tell me about his antics and adventures and not being able to see him.

"I missed you so much, Mattie," Eric sobs into my shoulder as he clings to me like a baby koala. "Why did you leave me?"

Up close, I can see the scratches and bruises starting to form on Eric's arms from his accident, and I hold him closer. He could have killed himself...

"Don't leave me again, Mattie," he whimpers when the front door to the house opens again. "Please don't leave me alone."

At the look on Mr. Mendleton's face, I know I can't make that promise to Eric. I know I'm getting sent away again because this man holds my mother's livelihood in his hands. If I don't leave, he will follow through on his threat from years ago. My mother will be jobless and I will be so buried under lawsuits and debt that I'll never find employment beyond minimum wage.

Setting the boy back on his feet, I ignore the tears falling from his eyes, even as they are shredding my heart. Against my better judgment, I use my thumbs to wipe the tears from Eric's cheeks. Showing his father that I care about him will likely only make things worse.

"Sorry, kiddo," I say to him and watch the light fade from his eyes. "I'm only stopping in to get the last of my stuff from Mom's rooms so that I can finish my move for grad school."

And just like four years ago, I broke my word to the only person who has ever mattered to me other than my mother. The boy in my arms jerks away and takes off running around the house to the expansive backyard.

I want to stay. I want to tell his asshole father to go fuck himself, but instead I square my shoulders and level him with a stern gaze.

"You need to get his meds adjusted," I growl out to the

man in the doorway as soon as I know that Eric has run far enough away to not be listening. "He's obviously manic right now, so whatever he is on isn't working well enough."

"There is nothing wrong with my son other than being a spoiled, attention seeking brat," Mr. Mendleton replies before turning back into the house. "He doesn't need your help. God will correct him once he accepts that his behavior is unacceptable."

I am left staring at the front of the house as the sound of the deadbolt turning signals the end of my visit. The bastard took him off his medications.

Running back to Mom's little apartment in the staff quarters, I hurriedly scribble a note telling her I'll be staying with Jackson. I can't risk making things worse for Eric by being here.

"Is that why you weren't there for my graduation party?" Eric asks, breaking me out of my memory. "Your mom told me you were coming and I was so excited, but then you weren't there."

I pull him tighter against me and try to explain.

"Your father's attorney sent me an email after Mom invited me on your orders. I was allowed to be there for an hour. I even snuck up to your rooms, but I thought I'd lost my little unicorn boy."

27

ERIC

He was there? How did I not know that?

Wait a second...

"Did you leave me a card?" I ask him as something is tickling at the edge of my memories. Father was talking about a card to someone on the phone after the party was over. His confused nod is the confirmation I needed for my brain to finally start to make sense of the memory.

"I wrote one to explain everything, to tell you that you were welcome to hang out with me in Boston if you still planned to go to Harvard. I had just gotten a job as a junior professor at one of the smaller colleges up there. I missed you so much, but when I saw your rooms and how they were so very much *not you*, I freaked out and dropped the card in your trash can.

"I regretted it the next day, but by then, the lawyers had descended and told me that I could not be within three hundred yards of the property and that if I were to attempt to contact anyone of the Mendleton family, I would be forced to repay the debt immediately in addition to trespassing and harassment criminal charges. I was also told that my mother would face the same penalties, plus losing her job, if I ever tried to use her as an intermediary."

I'm pretty sure my mouth is hanging open wide enough to blow an elephant at this point. Matt was there? My mother told me she knew nothing when I asked her about why he didn't show, which I'm guessing is probably true. Father told me to forget childish notions of friendship and forced me to socialize with his business partners instead of letting me hang out with my friends from school.

Spencer was the only one there who seemed to genuinely give a shit about me not getting to enjoy my party. He kept joining me with the adults instead of splashing in the pool like the rest of them. Even he was shocked that Matt was a no show. He'd only been hearing me talk about the guy for years at that point.

"I heard Father on the phone in the lounge after the party. He had a card in his hand that I didn't remember seeing at the party," I tell Matt while I try to piece together the fuzzy memories. I was heavily medicated at that time in my life, so most things just blend together. "He was asking someone to head to Boston, but I don't remember much more. He was angry and I didn't want to deal with him anymore. I barely managed to convince him to let me live in the dorms at Hawkins, I was afraid to risk him pulling that little bit of freedom away from me."

Matt pushes me to sit up and turns me to look at him. "Didn't you go to Pitt? I saw the acceptance letter on your desk."

Chuckling, I lean in to give him a kiss on the cheek before laying down to put my head in his lap. "Pitt was *my* choice, but Hawkins is more exclusive and looks better on a resume. Or at least that's what he said. I was tired of being stereotyped for being a rich kid, but I just went with what my father wanted to be able to get away from that house.

"It wasn't bad though. I somehow eventually ended up rooming with Steve who was there on scholarship. His girlfriend, now wife, Jen went to Pitt and lived off campus. I got to be a regular college student thanks to them... Well, at least for a little while..."

"Do you want to tell me about it?" Matt asks gently while running his fingers through my turquoise strands. "I got the overview from the article, but if you ever want to share the details, I'm here to listen. I'm never leaving you again."

Instead of telling him anything, I just nod and reach for the remote on the coffee table. Turning on Netflix, I pick out a movie for us to relax to. I'm not ready to share this with him just yet, but for the first time in five years, I feel safe... safe enough to remember everything, on my terms.

As the opening credits for Sherlock Holmes with Robert Downey Jr and Jude Law start to play, I let my mind drift back to five years ago.

28

ERIC

Five Years Ago:

It figures that I can finally legally drink, but I have zero desire to do so. Yesterday was my twenty first birthday, and just to hold to my life's shitty pattern, midterms. I know I aced them all, but it's still hard to fight off the adrenaline crash after testing.

"Bi-Polar disorder with Hyperactive-Impulsive ADHD" is my official diagnosis. It took crashing my car into the fountain for my father to finally recognize that I, in fact, needed those pills that my high school tutor Miss Melanie was getting for me. She thought she was giving me a bit of extra focus, but in reality she was helping my brain function closer to normal than it ever had before.

Unfortunately, my father took it to the extreme and had his family doctor over-medicate me. I was a fucking zombie for my last two years of high school into my freshman year of college. Much to my father's dismay, the medications did not cure the gay away even if they did take away all of the joy from my life.

After having to visit the clinic on campus for a case of strep throat, I found out that I don't have to go through my father's physicians to get my medical care. Through the assistance of some friends in the dorm, I found out about free clinics all over the county for people who do not have insurance. While I could easily afford to pay the fees associated with care, my father's accountant would surely flag the purchase and it would defeat the purpose of seeking my own care.

The next week, I sought out an independent, low cost psychologist and have been in control of my medications ever since. It has taken me almost two years to get my meds properly adjusted to where I feel like a normal human being, and now I'm going to be able to get into some night clubs to truly live for the first time in my life.

"Yo! King!"

I lift my head from the arm of the sofa where I was sprawled out waiting for my roommate to finish with his girlfriend upstairs. Felix throws his backpack onto the floor and holds his hand out for one of those weird bro hand slap shake things. Reaching my hand up, I let him do whatever he wants before he collapses into the ratty old leather recliner next to the stairs.

The guys who hang around with my roommate have taken to calling me "King" lately. Felix apparently fell asleep with the television on and when he woke up it was on a show about the Old Norse meanings of names. Apparently, Eric translates into the sole ruler, so he started to call me King and it just caught on within this crowd. I kinda like it.

"You coming to the party tonight?" he asks as he pulls off his hoodie to reveal the muscles underneath. I swallow the saliva that pools in my mouth before I start drooling and give myself away. One good thing about my current cocktail of medications is that I don't get spontaneous boners anymore.

"Um, I don't think so," I say as the sounds of the squeaky bedframe increase in frequency. "Steve and Jen are probably gonna call it a night after this, so it looks like the dorm and some alone time for me tonight."

Felix reaches over to shake my shoulder and the heat of his hand makes me forget the meds for a second while I have to force my dick to cooperate. These guys don't know I'm gay. No one at school knows except for Jen, and I only told her so she'd stop trying to set me up with her friends.

"You got me and the boys, dude! You need to get out and have fun for once in your life. Make Daddy's money pay to cover up a scandal or something. You need to get out there and meet more people than just us."

What Felix doesn't know is that I do technically have friends outside of him and his roommates. The three guys and two girls who share this house are far from my only friends, well more like acquaintances really. I only have maybe one friend, if he will still talk to me. Spencer and I haven't really spoken since my high school graduation party. We ended up at different schools, so I kinda lost my only real friend.

"Yeah, okay," I begrudgingly agree. "I guess it won't

hurt to go hang out with some new people. What's the party?"

Felix leans forward as I sit up and starts to fill me in on the details. I'm not going to get changed or anything, but he decides to run up and shower before we leave. As predicted, Steve and Jen stay behind while I head off to a party, squashed into the backseat of a 2009 Chevrolet Aveo between Felix and his currently off again girlfriend Tiffany. The long ride ends well after I wanted it to, and I'm surprised to see the party is not in Oakland, but well away from the campus in a neighborhood I know I have never even seen. I think my watch alone is worth more than some of these houses.

"Where are we?" I ask Tiff when Felix and the others pour into the house. I think the only reason she is still at the car is because she doesn't want to walk in with her ex.

"It's a party house for the hockey team," she tells me, hooking her arm in mine to pull me up the walk. "They can't get caught drinking on campus or the coach will kick them off the team, so one of the alumni bought this house for them to go nuts in exchange for continuing to win championships."

Walking in the front door, I'm hit with a wall of sound and ugh... smell. Tiff giggles at the look on my face which I can only assume is conveying the sheer disgust I feel regarding such a pungent aroma.

"The point is to get extremely drunk so you stop caring about the smell," she yells to be heard over the music. "Hockey sweat is somehow so much worse than any other *sport funk, but I would get railed by any member of the team cuz FFFFUUUUCK are those boys F.I.N.E. fine."*

Throwing my head back, I let loose a laugh that I haven't felt in a while. Tiff just pulls me farther into the house to the kitchen and grabs drinks for the both of us. I wave the cup away from me and she cocks an eyebrow in question.

Leaning in close to her ear, I tell her I can't mix alcohol with my meds. When I stand up straight again, I look down at her surprised face. I guess I don't really advertise that I take medications, but is it really all that shocking in this day and age that someone is medicated for something? This is the age of prescription throwbacks for doctors after all.

Tiff pulls me down so she can whisper into my ear, like she doesn't want anyone else to listen in.

"Don't freak out or anything if I'm wrong, but I think you just pinged my gay-dar."

I can't even stand up before I start laughing uncontrollably. Resting my forehead on Tiffany's shoulder, I let loose all of my tension and relax into the idea that it's not the end of the world if people find out at this point. I was out in high school. I can finally free myself of the last of my father's shackles and be the real me for my senior year of college.

"Yeah, you're not wrong," I tell her as I pour some Sprite into a cup from the counter full of mixers. "Let's go check out some cute hockey butts while you get wasted, and I'll be your sober eyes so you don't have to worry about beer goggles tonight."

29

ERIC

Five Years Ago: Continued

Two hours later, I am staring at the absolute treasure of a backside of the man currently carrying Tiffany upstairs to have his way with her, fully consensually of course. Tiff stopped drinking after one beer as soon as she realized no one was pressuring me about my non-drinking.

Sipping my now extremely flat pop, I glance around to see a lot of highly intoxicated people and a few rather shady looking guys prowling the exterior of the room. What I don't see is a single person I really know outside of recognizing their face from around the campuses. Felix, Adam, and Jeff are nowhere to be found. Glancing out the window, I notice Adam's car is no longer parked out front.

Great. Just my fucking luck. The guys abandoned me and Tiff in this crack house in the middle of the fucking slums, and now I'm going to have to sit around and wait for Tiff to finish getting her brains fucked out by a hockey god before I can order a rideshare. I'm not going to abandon her like her ex did. I understand now why Felix is always fucking single.

What the fuck is that stain in the corner? I'm going to fucking kill him when we get back to the house.

Taking another sip of my warm and flat root beer, I decide to chug it to avoid the hideous aftertaste I'm getting. No more dark drinks. Hell, I think I need to switch to water. I'm pretty sure the heat from so many bodies in such a small space is getting to me.

On the way to the counter with the mixers, a dizzy spell hits me out of nowhere. I grab for the counter to steady myself. That was weird. Maybe my sugar is low? When did I last eat? Wait, I've been drinking pure sugar... Can high blood sugar make you dizzy?

I feel an arm come around my waist and turn my head to see a rather brutish looking man holding me upright. I give him a grateful smile and try to tell him to just help me outside, but I find that the words aren't coming out.

Another guy comes up on my other side as they carry me out of the room. A few people I recognize ask if I'm alright as we go past, and I want to scream at them that I am NOT fucking alright. All I can do is whimper with no one hearing while the guys say they're going to take me upstairs to sleep it off.

I'm thrown roughly onto a bed and I can do nothing, say nothing, while my clothes are removed and the number of hands on me increases from two to four to six to who knows...

The voices in the room are loud yet muffled.

Their faces are clear, but I have no clue who they are.

"Sabrina only said to get him drunk," one guy says from where I assume the door is. I don't see who it is. I can't even move my head to look. "Why the fuck are you messing around like this? This is going too far. I'm calling an ambulance."

I can hear something that sounds like a slap and something hitting the wall before the hands are back on me and the faces are swimming in front of me again.

"Donny just got his ass benched for next season," the man who first grabbed me says to the others in the room before leering down at me. "This little faggot is begging for it. So we're going to be nice and give him what he wants so that bitch gets what she wants later and we get the dough."

My fear bleeds to the background and I start to feel a sort of numbness creep over me. The hands hurt me, but I can't react. The assholes rub me raw trying to get me erect. You would think a bunch of guys would understand the importance of lube, but they don't seem all that bright.

They finally give up on getting me hard when my fingers start to twitch instead of my dick. I feel strange being thankful when they flip me over onto my stomach. I probably should have hidden the fact that whatever they used on me was wearing off already. Maybe then I could have braced for it.

Pain unlike anything I could have ever conceived tears through my body and it burns through the rest of the drugs holding my voice captive. A scream rips from my throat, but before I can think enough to form words, someone's funk drenched cock gets shoved in my mouth.

Between the pain and the lack of air, I lose consciousness. When I come to, I don't know how long I was out or what else happened to me. I don't even know how many guys did anything to me. How many guys are on a hockey team?

I lurch over the side of the bed and vomit the contents of my stomach onto the filthy floor. Opening my eyes, I can see puddles of a viscous substance that I don't want to think too deeply on. How many times did I throw up in this exact place before awareness came back to me? Are all those puddles vomit or are they... from the monsters in the room?

The door slams open and shadowed in the doorway is one of the very few people in this world that I know would never hurt me. Spencer Wright looks like he's gone a couple rounds with someone, but he looks like a fucking superhero to me right about now.

He's too late to be the hero, but I know he won't let them touch me again. He'll protect me.

30

MATT

It's obvious to me that Eric isn't watching the movie. He's thinking through something. As a kid, it was one of my favorite things to watch. His mind is a thrilling place where he can make connections between things in minutes that would take most people ages to figure out. I've often wished my brain could take the same shortcuts his does, but today is not one of those days. He looks tormented.

"Cutie? Are you alright?" I ask, pausing the movie. I give his hair a little tug to make him look at me. His eyes are haunted. Leaning down, I place a kiss on his forehead. I'm sure we brought up some not so good memories for him today, but I want to make sure going forward that we are actually moving forward. We can't get trapped in the past.

"I love you, Mattie," he says as he snuggles back down on my lap. "Tomorrow is the fifth anniversary of...

the event... I haven't really faced it before today, not really."

Pulling the blanket off the back of the futon, I tuck it in around him and continue to stroke his hair. I only found out about what happened to him this morning. He's been living with it for five years. I know only general statements. He has vivid and explicit details. It's tearing me apart inside, so what is it doing to him?

"What can I do to help?" I ask him softly. I need to do something to make this right for him. I can't change the past, but I have to try to make his future brighter.

"Just be here, Mattie. Let me be your unicorn boy again," he tells me with a sad smile. Turning back toward the television, he grabs the remote from my hand to press play on the movie. I barely hear the whisper. "Don't let me go, Super Mattie."

Somehow I manage to keep my silent tears from falling on my boy as he drifts off to sleep with his head in my lap. Despite the fact that I have a class to teach at ten tomorrow morning, I refuse to move from where I am until I absolutely need to. This precious man still thinks I'm his hero.

"Super Mattie and Sparkles to the rescue!"

I can't stop my lips from quirking up at the call to arms from the seven year old at my side. I was teaching him how to play catch when the baseball ended up rolling into the rose bushes, his mother's prize winning rose bushes.

"Easy there, Sparkles," I tell him, restraining him by

grabbing the back of his shirt when he tries to dive after the ball. "We can't damage your mother's flowers"

Turning to me, his bottom lip quivers. "B-but what about the b-b-ball? I don't want to be done playing base-m-ball with you."

An athlete he is not, but I love that he tries so hard just for me. Seeing the tears start to form in his eyes, I know what I have to do. Ruffling his curls, I get down in the mulch and slowly army crawl between the bushes and the wall of the garage.

Mom is going to be pissed with how filthy I'm getting, but it's better for the kid of the cook to be dirty than their precious showpiece. Thorns from the rose bushes tear at my clothes and exposed skin, but I can see the ball just ahead. Snatching it up, I decide it's safer to keep going forward instead of trying to move backward or turning around.

"Mattie?" Eric's worried voice calls out from behind me, but I don't stop moving. His sniffles make me move even faster.

When I reach the end of the wall, I crawl out of the mulch and jump to my feet. I raise the hand holding the baseball in triumph as my little buddy sprints around the bushes to wrap his arms around my middle. The warmth I feel from his hug makes it easy to ignore the small pains and itches from the scratches on my left side.

"Super Mattie..."

Happy memories from our joint childhood run through my mind until I drift off into my own slumber. My dreams are all the good times we shared while we both grew up. I was his superhero, saving his toys from the perils of the vacuum while Eliza cleaned the third floor of the house. I was his chaperone on his "adventures" while I would run errands for my mom. I was his comfort when his father decided he was too old for what he called baby toys and threw out all of his stuffed animals.

My alarm going off in the bedroom jolts me awake before my dreams have the chance to take a darker turn. The first thing I notice is the stabbing pain in my neck from falling asleep sitting upright on the futon. Thirty two is well beyond the "I can sleep in any position" phase of my life. As I try to massage the crick out of my neck, I look around and realize Eric isn't in the room. Before I can panic, I hear whispered expletives coming from the hallway.

"Will you shut the fuck up, you stupid machine?!" he hisses as I head down the hallway toward my bedroom. "Where is the fucking off button?"

My cock definitely takes notice of the nearly naked man standing in front of my dresser, dripping water on my carpet. I'm a little disappointed he decided to take a shower without me, but we *have* only been together for about a day.

"You have to hold two buttons at the same time for at least ten seconds, otherwise it's just a snooze for ten minutes," I tell him, making him scream and drop the towel he had loosely wrapped around his waist. I chuckle at his reaction. "Good morning to you, too."

I walk up to my dresser to turn off the alarm. It's a

struggle to not smirk at the glare being leveled at me from the naked turquoise haired drowned rat before he turns to pick up his towel. I might have stopped the smirk, but nothing could've stopped the groan that escapes when I catch a glimpse of his pucker as he bends over.

The little minx shakes his ass before standing back up to look at me. I love the sultry smirk that blooms on his face as he tosses the towel over his shoulder and sashays his way out of my bedroom. Giving me a wink at the door, he disappears into my bathroom, and I hear the shower start back up. Shaking my head, I pull out a fresh pair of underwear and t-shirt for an undershirt.

When I reach my closet, I see that I have limited options for what to wear today. Most of the time, I grab a random button down and pair of slacks. I don't even know if I match half the time. Will Eric care if I look like a bum? Probably, but I'm sure he will find a way to be my stylist going forward, just like he did for me when I started high school. He took over picking out my outfits every day for my entire freshman year before he deemed me proficient enough to be left unsupervised.

Turning away from my closet, I figure I can at least get coffee started. I've never worried about fashion for work before, but then again I've never had anyone to worry about what they think about how I look before.

As I scoop the grounds into the filter, I pause.

I've never had anyone to look good for? Didn't I care about how I looked for Sylvia?

Putting the carafe under the spout, I hit the button to

start the brew. The realization hits me like a freight train. I never actually cared about what Sylvia thought. We basically just coexisted for our entire relationship. I mean, we talked and went on dates, but it was all perfunctory. Even the sex was merely mediocre.

Cocking my head, I listen for the shower. Estimating that I have at least ten minutes based on the number of skin care products I saw on my dresser top, I grab my phone to call Syl. I feel like I owe her an apology for wasting so many years of her life.

31

MATT

At seven on a Monday morning, Sylvia should be on her way to Salem for a meeting. It's the only day of the week that she has to drive, so I know I'll catch her alone. This is a conversation that has needed to happen.

"Hey Lew," she says cheerfully. "I was going to call you later today."

Taken aback, I almost miss my mug while pouring my coffee. Putting the carafe back so the rest of the pot can brew, I take a sip before answering.

"Hey Syl. Whatcha need from me?"

She hesitates for about ten seconds before she says, "I was thinking that we should give us another chance."

Involuntarily, I spit coffee across the kitchen. Still choking and coughing from the shock of her statement, I put the phone down on the counter to grab a paper towel.

"We were good together, Lewis. Good enough you asked me to marry you. I freaked out when you said you weren't coming home after your mom got better. I thought you'd fight for us. I was just being chicken shit about moving away from home. I miss you, Lew. I still want to marry you."

The gasp from across the room makes me turn fast enough that I knock my almost full cup of coffee off the countertop to shatter on the linoleum below. I didn't realize I had put the phone on speaker when I set it down.

Smashing my finger on the screen to end the call, I call out to Eric when he races back toward the bedroom. I can hear my phone ringing in the kitchen, but I ignore it. Sylvia is over nine hours away. She doesn't matter. Eric does.

Knocking on the bedroom door, I call out to my boy. It takes a while for him to open the door for me, but when he does, he immediately turns away from me.

"I won't be your little secret," he says and sits on the edge of the bed before I can say anything. "I get that people can love more than one person, but that's not me. I love you, Mattie, but I won't share you. I don't like ultimatums, but it's gotta be her or me, Mattie. You have to choose, and you have to do it now before I fall any more in love with you."

I fall to my knees in front of my brave boy. He's put his heart out there, and there's only one way I know of to reward him. Grabbing his chin, I pull gently until he's looking at me.

"It's Super Mattie and Sparkles forever," I whisper,

my lips brushing against his. "You've always held my heart, my precious unicorn boy."

I give him my heart all over again with the kiss I place on his lips. I only want to make him mine in every way possible.

Standing slowly, I don't break our kiss, pushing my boy to lie back on the bed. Using my left hand to keep my weight off his upper body, my right travels from his throat in a gentle caress down his torso to the waistband of my favorite pajama pants.

"I thought I have shit taste in fashion?" I ask him as I pull the drawstring to loosen the pants.

The look Eric gives me is a mix of mischief and something more special.

"I guess it's a good thing that I was the one who picked these out, isn't it?"

Chuckling at his cheeky response, I give the pants a yank and delight in the squeak of surprise I get from my boy before I start kissing my way up his thigh. I've decided this very special and unique boy deserves some very special kisses today.

"Mattie..."

Eric's groan encourages me as I reach my goal. I might have never sucked a dick before, but I have watched more than enough of my share of porn to know of most of the techniques... and I may have practiced with some popsicles over the last week after getting my first glance of him at Pegasus.

Wrapping my right hand around his base, I slowly stroke him in a loose grip while my left hand moves to fondle his balls. Watching his face, he seems confused but enraptured with what I'm doing.

Has no one ever done this for his pleasure before?

Lowering my mouth to the head of his penis, I lick up the precum that has started to flow and delight in the sounds I'm able to pull from my boy. I want to surprise him, so I remove my right hand and work my way down his shaft, an inch at a time, keeping eye contact the entire time.

My own dick is dripping in my sweats as I work my way to swallowing around the head of Eric's cock. His head flies back and he grips the bedsheets desperately when I swallow around him a second time. I want his nails digging into me, not the sheets. I want him to mark me, bruise me, bleed me, claim me.

Pulling up, I switch to shallow suction as I thrust my tongue onto his slit over and over. Based on the sounds coming from my cutie, I've found something he really likes.

"Mattie... I'm... Don't stop... Gonna..."

I want his release. I want to take in every part of him. Intellectually, I know I shouldn't be giving head without a condom, but this is Eric. I don't want anything to come between us, not anymore.

Impatient for my reward, I move my left hand and push my middle finger against his tight pucker while my thumb presses against his taint. The combination of those with my suction seems to be the right recipe for release because I have to start swallowing a second later. Someday soon, I want to know what a facial would feel like, but this morning, I just want to consume my boy.

Pulling off his spent dick, I pull the Grinch up to cover him back up.

"Such a good boy for me, Sparkles," I whisper and lay down next to him to wait for him to ride out the afterglow.

32

ERIC

I really had no intention of making Matt late for work today. I actually planned on making him breakfast and giving him a massage before he had to leave for campus. His flaky bitch of an ex made that plan fly out the window.

I hope she *is* dumb enough to show up here. Then I could drown her in the Mon and let the mutant fish eat her corpse.

Chuckling at how vicious my mind seems to go with my jealousy, I pull into my designated spot at the Monarch Room. Clarence pulled me aside last night and apologized to me for pulling the rug out from under me with his whole no planned show stunt. The guys in the audience that night were apparently there to fuck with Nick in particular. He works a few jobs and they had apparently been showing up everywhere he was to harass him.

To protect Nick, and any of the rest of us who were

spotlight acts, he took the headliners show off the schedule. Instead of highlighting who is performing each night on the website, we're switching to having themed shows. He's decided on a theme for next month's feature show, and he wants me to help pick the musical numbers for all of us.

"Mama, I'm hoooome!"

My voice echoes in the empty club as the door slams behind me. After Matt left at nine fifty five this morning, I took another shower before making myself absolutely fabulous. If I have to face this day, I'm going to be fierce while I do it. Finding my gold manties in his underwear drawer was a pleasant surprise, and I slipped them on for a physical reminder of my Mattie as I try to get through today without panicking.

"Get back here, Brat," Clarence calls out from the sound booth room above the bar. "I've narrowed down our choices, but I need your input for assigning who gets what song and what version we want to use."

Curious, I drop my adorbs blue plaid Coach mini backpack behind the bar and race up to the little room to join Clarence and our sound guru Felicia. The two of them are sitting in front of her laptop and it looks like they've compiled a Spotify playlist.

"The theme is going to be 'Love Yourself' and a lot of these songs reflect that in a way," Felicia says as she rolls her chair back from the sound table. "We just can't agree on the flow of the show."

"Are we telling a story over the entire show or is each number a story?" I ask while scrolling through the songs.

I see a few that fit where I am now, but I kind of want to let our patrons know that we aren't always all sunshine and rainbows.

"I kind of think we should embrace the club name and show the metamorphosis. A lot of people are still stuck in the hating themselves phase and I think this could show them that there is a way out of it."

"That's the whole point of this lineup," Clarence insists. "We need to show that positivity."

Rolling her eyes, Felicia turns to me. I see she understands what I'm talking about.

"We can't just show the end result. We need to give them the visual of the darkness so they know they aren't alone," I tell him as I start searching for a song.

Felicia stops him from interrupting with a hand on his arm.

"Some of us are only starting to come out of the darkness, and I don't want to be performing a lie anymore."

I hit play and the song *Two Steps Away* by Heading North starts playing through the club. I let the song echo through the empty space while Felicia turns to me wide eyed. Tears fall from Clarence's eyes as the chorus hits.

I'M ALWAYS
TWO STEPS AWAY FROM
FEELING OKAY
IT'S BETTER THIS WAY,
I WANNA LIKE MYSELF

Don't ask for the stars
They're too far away
I guess the dirt is okay
I wanna like myself

He pulls me into a fierce hug as the tears fall from his eyes. I let my friend sob into my shoulder as the lyrics wash over me. This song was probably the first time I've ever felt like someone out there understood that loving myself is impossible.

"I think this would be a good intro song," I tell him when he pulls back. "They're a local band. They're queer. And we need to start to normalize that loving yourself might be too unattainable for a lot of people. We need to start with like."

"Where did you hear that song?" Felicia asks as she adds it to the playlist for the new show in the intro position.

"It was playing at a restaurant I stopped at after a date."

I don't want to explain I heard it after getting a quickie in a dingy bathroom at a bar in Oakland. I'm still kind of afraid I traumatized the poor guy when I burst into tears while he was pulling up his pants. It's kind of overwhelming the first time you feel like you're not alone in your pain.

Clarence pats me on the back as he sits back in his chair. I feel pride bloom inside of me from that simple gesture. Staring at the back of his head, I realize that he has become my surrogate parental figure. He's not only my drag mother, he has protected me and supported me from the day we met. He's been the bitch and the rules guy so that I could relieve some of the pressure.

How did I not see this sooner?

"Thank you," I whisper in his ear as I throw my arms around his neck from behind to give him a hug. "Thank you for saving me."

Patting my hands to release him, I ignore the sniffles he's still trying to stifle as he says, "Alright, we have our intro. What about the rest?"

We spend the next three hours choosing songs. Clarence even agrees that this show is going to feature some of our kings as well as us queens. Drag is not an exclusive thing for only one gender. Drag is an expression that we want to share with the world. I'm surprised that I'm getting the feature for both the intro and the closer.

"Are you sure you want me as the closer before the finale? That's Cleo's spot."

Clarence looks at me with a soft smile before he tells me, "Cleo is stepping down next month to be able to plan a wedding."

Felicia and I both squeal in delight when he flashes the diamond ring on his left hand. It's not that flashy, but it suits him. Cleo might be flashy, but Clarence is classy.

"Theo has shit taste in men, but he's good at picking out jewelry," I tease and dodge the subsequent swing at my head. We giggle and ogle the ring for a few minutes when it hits me.

"If Cleo is stepping back, who is going to be running the ship? I'm not listening to Fred or Malcolm. Hell; I barely listen to you."

Felicia wraps me in a hug from behind while I try to wrap my mind around the answer that comes out of this asshole's mouth.

"I think it's time for Sassy to run the show."

33

ERIC

As soon as the shock wore off, Clarence took me to the office to fill out the necessary paperwork to promote me to club manager while he keeps his position as director and talent management. Over the next month he is going to train me on all of the ins and outs of the business side of things, but I already know most of it from my almost three years of college.

Letting myself back into Matt's trailer using the keypad on the backdoor, I plop myself on his bed to contemplate everything. I parked my mini in the yard next to my truck. Something is itching at the back of my mind, telling me to keep it hidden that I'm here. The grin that hasn't left my face for the last hour turns downright devious as I glance at the clock on Matt's dresser.

Three forty two.

The class he has with Toby starts at four. Let's see if I can get him all worked up and make our puppy be naughty...

Kink Manor Queenie:
Can I be teacher's pet?

Mattie Cakes:
Do I get to put a collar on my pet?

HOLY FUCK!

I shoot up to a sitting position while my dick is trying to reach outer space. I was only kidding, but hot damn, ain't no way I'd say no to a very visual claim placed by him.

Kink Manor Queenie:
U know what that means?

Don't tease me

Mattie Cakes:
I know what it means. I want everyone to know you are mine.

I don't share either

Kink Manor Queenie:
SWOON

I was gonna send a naughty pic to distract you for class but you just beat me at my game

Mattie Cakes:
Send it anyways. I need to see my Cutie

Opening the camera app, I take a silly selfie next to the painting I gave him when I was still a kid. I didn't say it would be a dirty pic. I hit send and collapse back onto the bed in giggles. Imagine him sitting at his desk, fighting a boner in anticipation of a dick pic and then gets that.

Mattie Cakes:.
There's my Cutie.

Your Mattie loves it. But you're heading for a spanking if you keep teasing me.

Send me a dirty one for after class.

I want my naughty unicorn

Holy Mary, mother of sweet baby Jesus! That man should not be that sexy over text.

Closing out my text messages, I go to the living room to grab some more sexy panties out of my suitcases. I know I have a glitter rainbow lace thong in there somewhere that will be perfect for Mattie's naughty unicorn, especially if I have a spanking to look forward to.

That reminds me...

I change my contact name from Kink Manor Queenie to Sparkles the Unicorn. I can't wait to answer questions on that one later in the KM chat. Story time with Sassy is one of Lucky's favorite things to do, and Sparkles has a ton of stories that I can tell without feeling sad now that Mattie is back in my life.

Changing into my thong, I go into the bathroom to glam up a bit more. Super Mattie needs his Sparkles. After all, what's a hero without his sidekick?

Glancing at the clock when I get back to the bedroom, it is now four twenty three. Class is in session for another twenty two minutes, so I fire off three different shots. The full body one was a bit difficult to figure out positioning since I have no clue where my selfie stick disappeared to in my impromptu move, but the other two were easily accomplished.

My phone going off at four thirty surprises me. Matt told me he is adamant about not checking his phone during class. Opening the messages app, I collapse back onto the bed in laughter.

Pan Pup:
What the fuck did you do to my professor?

> **Sparkles the Unicorn:**
> I thought he doesn't check messages during class

Pan Pup:
He doesn't. But he's had to adjust himself twice since his alert went off.

I can't afford to fail this class dude. Can't you sext him during his other classes?

> **Sparkles the Unicorn:**
> Sorry Pup. I'll keep it to his other classes. Now get off your phone and pay attention or I'll tattle to the teacher

Pan Pup:

Tossing my phone to the side, I grab the blanket to

cover up a bit. I don't want to have to get dressed just to have Mattie do more work after such a long day. At some point I must have dozed off because I swear I only closed my eyes for a second and suddenly it's dark outside.

Wrapping the blanket around me like a cloak, I wander to the kitchen to grab something to eat. Mattie offered to close his office hours today to come home right after his class with Toby, but I told him I'd be fine. I can wait until after eight to see my lover. Glancing at the clock on the microwave, I've got about an hour to go.

Oooh. He's got the stir fry noodle thingies. Toby is always hoarding those anytime they end up at Kink Manor. I grab a Korean BBQ one, add water, and put it in the microwave for the required four minutes. It might not be the most nutritious meal, but I missed lunch and need to eat something to take my evening meds.

As soon as the microwave goes off, I grab a fork and head to the futon with my meal. Wrapped up in the comfy blanket, I wiggle in happiness as I pull up Netflix to enjoy dinner and a movie. I just need to get Mattie to invest in some chopsticks for next time. It feels weird eating noodles like this with a fork.

The sound of the backdoor lock beeping has me almost choking on my slurp of noodles. Looking at the clock in the kitchen, I realize Mattie isn't supposed to be home yet. If that man ditched work after being late, I swear I'll be beating *his* ass. And it won't be a funishment if I have to do it.

Jumping up to rip him a new one, I immediately fall back to the futon in surprise. It's not Matt. It's some woman I've never met, and she is looking at me like I'm dirt under dog shit.

"Who the fuck are you to be in my fiancé's home?" she demands of me. "Get out before I call the police!"

Tucking myself into the blanket as much as I possibly can, I try to understand what she said.

"Mattie is at work and didn't tell me he was having visitors," I tell her as I try to slide by to get some clothes to put on, but she pushes me back down on the futon. For a woman, she's got a lot more strength than I was expecting.

"Oh, how cute," she sneers at me. "Lewis decided to experiment and found himself a pet fag for a few weeks. Well guess what, sweetheart. He doesn't care about you. He couldn't even be bothered to give you a real name. So get the fuck out of our home."

The woman is seriously fucked in the head. I thought my brain was twenty kinds of fucked up, but this lady's takes it to a whole new level.

"Sylvia, I take it?" I ask her when she turns to head toward the bedroom. I'll be damned if I let her into the space where Mattie and I made love less than twelve hours ago. "I seem to recall you dumped your Lewis and left him homeless because you weren't willing to sacrifice even a fraction of your life for him to support his only family. Why do you think he'd take back a selfish bitch like you?"

Her screech of rage is the only warning I get before she pounces on me.

34

MATT

It's a struggle not to race home as soon as I pull up the pics that Eric sent during my last class. Unfortunately, Mondays are my office hours and Eric made me promise to stay the whole time since he made me late for my first class this morning. I really wish I didn't make that promise. Staring at my phone I chuckle.

> **Sparkles:**
> You have the new manager of the Monarch Room in your bed waiting for you so don't make me wait too long

Of course, he had to add the extra bit of good news at the end to really make me want to celebrate his promotion. Maybe, I'll swing by the store and pick up the stuff for some root beer floats? He got me hooked on them with using coffee ice cream when he grabbed the wrong carton out of the freezer on his tenth birthday.

I alternate between the live feed in my living room

and those texts. Only my naughty unicorn would be eating noodles practically naked on my futon.

"Professor Barnes?"

I look up from my phone to see the campus bakery owner in the doorway holding a cup of coffee and a bag that smell suspiciously like his double chocolate muffins.

"What's up, Donnie?" I ask him as I subtly adjust myself under my desk. I have a little over an hour to go until I can go home, so I might as well hang out with him. He's one of the few guys on campus that I have had regular interactions with since I'm a younger professor and trying to avoid fraternization issues. The guys from the house are going to be testing those waters enough for me, now.

"You know the Mendleton family, right?" he asks as he sets the bag and coffee down on my desk. "I need to get a message to the son, Eric, but everything I've tried has come up undeliverable. I really hope you can help me out here. It's important."

It's difficult to contain my anger at his asking about my Cutie the day after the media threw him to the wolves, but I somehow reign it in enough to ask through clenched teeth, "I haven't spoken to anyone with that last name in almost a decade. Why do you need to get in touch with him?"

Don's shoulders fall as he slumps down in the chair. The disappointment rolling off of him is practically suffocating.

"I don't know if you read the news or anything, but this thing happened five years ago and a really nasty guy is getting a parole hearing thanks to a loophole his piece of shit lawyer used in appeal. I'm testifying to the parole board, but basically without Eric, the chances are pretty high that his ass will be walking out of jail."

Something is niggling at the back of my mind, but I push past it to ask.

"Why would you be testifying?"

"I was on the hockey team with the guy," he says with a sigh. "I tried to stop them that night, but after they slapped me around, I crawled out of the room to try to find someone else who could help. I blacked out after falling down the stairs, and by the time I came to, it was too late.

"I fucking failed him once. I can't let that fucker get out to hurt him again, man. Please, Lew. If you can find him, tell him the hearing is in two weeks. Give him my number if he's willing to come. If he can't face Rafe, I know my lawyer can probably get approval for something remote. But I need to know by Friday. They're closing the witness list at three."

My phone dings to alert me that someone has unlocked my back door. I hold up a finger to let Donnie know I just have to check this out. I didn't get a notification of it being unlocked or locked again after Eric got back from his meeting with Clarence, so I need to know who the fuck just came into my home.

The code used to get into the house was my mother's birthday, which I set up solely for her use. I let out a breath of relief and prepare for my phone to ring with the admonishment from my mother at keeping Eric a secret.

Donnie gives me a questioning look when my smirk falls off my face. Mom would have called right away...

I pull up the doorbell camera for the backdoor and rewind it to see who came in and jump out of my chair.

"What's up, Lew?"

"Fuck, Donnie. I gotta go. Someone broke into my house and..."

"I'll follow you. Let's roll."

I grab his arm when we get to the parking lot and drag him to my car. I had pulled up the hidden camera on my TV and Sylvia is in my house with Eric only in his fucking underwear.

"I need you to watch this feed for me while I drive," I tell him as I shove my phone into his hand. "I need to know what is going on when I get there."

Starting the engine, I don't even look before racing out of the parking lot. It takes a second for me to realize I can hear the audio of the feed through my speakers. Thank fuck for Bluetooth. Turning up the dial, my stomach turns at what I'm hearing.

"Lewis decided to experiment and found himself a pet fag for a few weeks. Well guess what, sweetheart. He doesn't care about you. He couldn't even be bothered to give you a real name. So get the fuck out of our home."

I've never heard Sylvia sound so ugly. It's not just the words. It's the pure hatred behind them. How the fuck did I ever consider marrying her?

"Who the fuck is the crazy bitch?" Donnie asks me as I pass the BDSM club. I'm less than two minutes from home.

"My ex-fiancée," I tell him as I fishtail on the turnoff to head up the hill. "She told me this morning that she wants to get back together."

"I hope you told her fuck no," Donnie admonishes as he grabs onto the oh shit handle.

"That was the plan, but I had to reassure my boy when he heard her shit. I didn't think she'd drive the nine hours to finish the conversation from this morning."

I grimace over at him for making me miss Eric's reply, but then I hear an ungodly screech of rage coming from my speakers and I floor it through the entrance to the trailer park. I know I did some damage to my under-carriage and alignment going over the speed humps at this speed, but as I pull up to the trailer and turn off the car, I hear glass shattering from inside.

"Code is 0323," I call out to Donnie as he races to the front door. I head to the back. The door is still unlocked, so I'm able to get to the chaos much faster. As soon as I clear the hallway, it takes a few seconds to make sense of what I'm seeing.

Sylvia is on the floor, covered in what looks like noodles and Eric is standing over her holding her at fork point. I would love to appreciate his enthusiasm for wearing a glittery rainbow lace thong for me, but I really hate the fact that others are seeing him this exposed.

Donnie crashes through the front door and time restarts.

"What the fuck?"

As soon as Donnie speaks, Eric's head jerks up to look at him. The fork moves away from Sylvia and he holds it out at the man in front of him while he warily backs away.

I probably should have announced myself before grabbing him. Instead, I end up with a fork stuck in my arm and my boy weeping into my chest.

35

ERIC

It took three hours to get everyone out after the cops came. Turns out Father Dearest was behind Sylvia the home-wrecker the whole time. The finance company she works for is a subsidiary of one of his companies. She was an intern when my father read Mattie's card. He had one of his guys pick her out and hired her on the expectation that she would seduce Matt to stay the fuck away from Pittsburgh, and by extension, me.

She sang like a fucking canary as soon as the cuffs went on her wrists. Matt looked sick. His friend looked angry. Something about his friend from the university sets my teeth on edge, but I am just chalking that up to what today is.

"What set you off with Donnie?" he asks me as he grabs a couple of pops out of the fridge. "You haven't reacted like that in front of me before."

I shrug and try to explain. "Ever since that... event... sometimes things will trigger my body to react. It could be something totally random like a specific song or like the smell of root beer. Something about the way he burst in and his voice combined to make my body remember before my mind could catch up."

Matt pulls me down on the futon next to him and says, "There's a good reason for that. Donnie is Donald Hastings, the player who got beat bloody that night for trying to stop his teammates when he found out what they planned to do to you."

"That was him?" I whisper incredulously. The man who stood up for me is still around. "Is he alright? I mean, they didn't permanently hurt him that night, right?"

Mattie hugs me tight and reassures me that his friend is fine, just worried about the parole hearing coming up.

"This is why I don't celebrate my birthday," I mumble into Matt's chest as he puts on the second season of Bridgerton to binge. I need him to catch up so we can escape into the exploits of the Ton and see what juicy gossip Lady Whistledown reveals next season. I still don't really understand the whole tree thing in the intro, but I start to relax into my lover's embrace as the scenes pop up on the bark of the tree.

"Hush and watch your show," he tells me with a kiss to the top of my head. "You're lucky you didn't get a spanking for breaking my favorite bowl."

"How did I manage to forget about the spanking?" I groan and sit up. "I was naughty. I deserve a spanking, Mattie."

Clucking his tongue, he pulls me back down to lay my head in his lap. Wracking my brain, I try to figure out how on earth I can finagle a spanking at this point. My dick is already excited for one, and I dressed up specifically to have my cheeks free for it.

Turning around to face his body instead of the television, I jerk in surprise at the thought that comes to me. *I actually want to perform oral.*

Matt glances down at my movement but turns his attention back to the screen. Moving slowly, I reach for the front of Matt's sweats to pull them down. He glances down again and shifts his hips with a smirk. Oh. My. God. He isn't going to stop me.

With more confidence, I pull his half hard cock out of his pants. *The fucker didn't bother putting on underwear!* Licking along his length, I realize it's not so bad. Slowly I pull him into my mouth and gently bob my head back and forth on his lap. I can feel him getting harder inside my mouth, and it triggers a mixture of feelings inside of me when his hand comes down on the back of my head.

"Stay still and keep me warm, Sparkles, my naughty unicorn," he says with a grin. "Let your Mattie watch his show in peace."

My eyes widen as I meet his gaze. We're doing cock-warming?!

Oh, I'm all fucking for this!

Settling in, I gently suckle on Matt while he pets me. Somehow, I seem to fade into a type of subspace, and I'm more relaxed than I've ever been in all of my times at the

Devil. Before I can make sense of it, Matt taps my cheek and I pull back off him.

"Time for bed, Cutie," he says as he turns off the television. I'm still half out of it as he tucks us into his bed, and we drift off to dreamland together.

I wake up the next morning to the smell of coffee and the delicious aroma elicits a groan from my throat. Naked coffee date sounds like a wonderful idea. Maybe, I can get some extra protein for breakfast this morning? Or maybe Mattie needs a boost in his protein intake?

I hear Matt in the kitchen talking to someone, but I can't figure out if he's on the phone or if yet another person has invaded our home. Looks like fully naked coffee needs to wait until I can ascertain if we're alone.

Our home? Even though it's only been a few days, this small trailer feels more like home than any place I've ever been. Mattie really better plan on keeping me here, cuz I'm not leaving.

I rush through my morning routine and throw on one of Matt's hoodies to cover myself enough for the sensibilities of anyone who has the audacity to invade at eight o'clock in the morning. As soon as I clear the hallway, I have two seconds to realize I should have found some pants before Matt's mother is crushing me in a hug.

"Oh, sweetie, I'm so happy you found him!" she calls back to Matt in the kitchen as she steers me to the stools for the breakfast bar. I'm extremely thankful that Matt likes really baggy hoodies and that the one I picked this morning is long enough to keep everything covered.

"It's good to see you again Ms. Sara," I mumble while

trying to keep the hoodie in place to hide my Sparkle thong.

"Pssh," she hisses as she grabs me for another hug. "Call me Mom."

I look at Matt in panic. What the fuck am I supposed to do? Do they even make manuals to tell you what to do when your lover's mother shows up while you're in your spank me thong and tells you to call her Mom?

36

MATT

The look on Eric's face has me almost snorting coffee up my nose. Taking pity on my cutie, I bring a cup of coffee over to him with a plate of my mother's French toast. When the news this morning reported on Sylvia's break in and Mr. Mendleton's involvement, she rushed over here. Luckily for us, she texted when she left, so I had time to get myself up and presentable. I decided to let Eric sleep so that I could prepare her for him being here.

"Mattie, why is this poor boy half naked? Do you need me to do your laundry so that he can put some pants on?"

Eric starts to choke on his bite of French toast, and my mother absently pounds on his back without removing her glare from my face. I'm torn between laughing and running as far as I fucking can from this situation. This is *not* how I expected to be coming out to my mother.

"Well you see, Eric and I are kind of... together, Ma," I

tell her and flinch in anticipation of the slap that I'm sure is coming. After a few seconds, I squint over at her to see a soft smile on her face instead of the outrage I was expecting.

It's not like I ever thought my mother is in any way intolerant, but she has been constantly reminding me that all of her friends are grandmothers now. Not to mention, the age difference. I mean, he was barely out of diapers when she started working for his family.

"Is that okay with you, Ms. Sara?" Eric asks sheepishly. "I've always loved Mattie, and now he loves me back."

The pain and fear in his voice breaks through my own nerves regarding my mother and I come around the counter to pull him into my arms.

"I've always loved you, Sparkles," I tell him with a kiss to his turquoise bedhead. "It's just the sexy stuff didn't show up until last week."

He lets out a soft giggle while my mother snorts into her coffee. "Seems you two don't need my blessing after all, but since you asked, sweetie, I'm ecstatic you two found your way to each other."

She puts a hand on each of our cheeks and gives us a smile before turning to put her coat on.

"Sorry I interrupted your little love nest and will give you more notice for my next visit. Eric, sweetie, let me know when you're free and we can go out for brunch to catch up."

Before she reaches the door, my brain catches up to everything that just happened.

"Don't you have anything to say about me liking men?"

I don't know why I'm so hung up on this, but I feel like I need to actually hear what she thinks about me not being straight.

"You don't need to put on a label or explain it to me, Mattie," she says as she opens the front door. "Love is what matters and you two have always had more than enough for each other."

I sink down onto the stool my mother had vacated when I hear her car pull away from the trailer. That wasn't the reaction I was expecting. I expected *something* more. I never thought she would be one of those parents who disowned their children for being queer, but I expected at least some confusion... especially after being engaged to a woman for the last three years.

Shit, was it really that long? That should have been a clue.

"Penny for your thoughts, good sir?" Eric asks with a horrid cockney accent as he pokes me in the ribs. "What's wrong?"

"She didn't care," I mutter as I get up to wash her dishes from breakfast. "I just came out to my mother, and she didn't react at all."

"I think she took it quite well, personally."

"Yeah, but I expected more of a reaction. I've spent the last few days trying to figure out how I could explain how I could make it thirty two years without even an inkling that I might not be straight. And she constantly mentions wanting grandkids, and now she won't get them. I mean it's not like I expected her to disown me or anything like your parents did, but I expected *something*."

Eric wraps his arms around my waist from behind me. Placing his chin on my shoulder he gives me a kiss to my neck for comfort while I finish up the breakfast dishes.

"I got a few things to say about that," he says as he lets me go to lean against the counter next to me. "Number one, don't assume because your closet was in a different house than mine, it wasn't just as hard for you to come out of it. Sharing your authentic self is one of the hardest things a person can do. I'm proud of you for choosing to tell the most important person in your life your truth.

"Number two. If that woman wants grandkids, we'll get her grandkids someday. I'm not sure how I feel about adopting a baby, but I've met my share of former foster kids at this point who could have used a bit more love in their lives. Let's give it a couple years before we take that leap."

Eric reaches over to turn off the water and pull me in front of him. "Number three. I don't care what surprises you discover about yourself or when they come to you. I've always loved you and will continue to do so even if you find out you were switched at birth with an alien. You are mine, Lewis Matthias Barnes, the Second, and God himself could never keep me away from you now that I've found you again."

All the pain and stress of the last few days rushes to the surface and I grab onto my boy like he's the last lifejacket on the Titanic. It all pours out of me and I weep on the shoulder of my precious unicorn boy. The guilt, the shame, the anger that I've directed at myself for taking that deal...

"I'm so sorry, Eric."

Pulling my face up so that he can see me, he whispers, "You have nothing to apologize for. You were a kid being blackmailed by a determined, crooked as fuck, asshole who wanted you out of the way."

Reaching up to wipe my tears, he says in a way too casual tone, "I have no doubt if you hadn't left on your own, he would have arranged an accident. I mean, hell, he managed to arrange an entire fucking relationship that almost ended up with you married to a fucking bigot."

I step back from him feeling a lot better. Yeah, his dad really fucked with my life for the last fifteen years, maybe even longer if I try to think on it.

"At least tell me the sex was good," Eric says and surprises a laugh out of me. "I mean, based on her personality and fashion sense, she has to have a golden pussy or something to keep a man like you tied down for five years."

"Seven," I choke out between breaths. "And no, it wasn't that good."

"Then why the fuck would you stay with her?!"

I finally get my breathing under control and step back into his space to wrap my arms around my cutie, my Sparkles, my unicorn boy.

"If I couldn't be with you, it didn't matter who I was

around. I think my head accepted her because it knew no one would ever have my heart. I think I stayed with her because I was afraid of finding someone else who would take up your place in my heart, and I knew deep down she was no competition."

"Super Mattie still got game," he chuckles before he leans in to kiss me.

It looks like I'm going to be late again today.

37

ERIC

Two Weeks Later:

"Are you sure you want to be in the same room as him?" the victim's advocate asks me for the fifteenth time since we entered this stupid sterile waiting room at the jail. "You have the right to testify from here and it will weigh just as heavily with the board."

I wish I could have Mattie here with me, but he's waiting outside with Spencer and Donnie. They have already given their testimony. The board seems to be trying to alternate between those of us who want to see Rafe Dennison rot in prison for the rest of his life and those who want him released. Unfortunately, there seems to be more witnesses for their side because this is taking forever.

"Alright, you're up," the squirmy little man tells me when the light above the far door starts to blink. "Last chance to do it remotely?"

I shake my head and approach the door. He pushes a

button and the door is pulled open by a guard on the other side. Taking a deep breath, I cross the threshold and come face to face with the monster who stars in every fucking nightmare I've had over the last five years.

Rafe Fucking Dennison is sitting handcuffed to a metal table. I'm kind of disappointed to see that he's wearing like grayish scrub looking clothes. I've been imagining him in orange which is so not his color, but I guess this works too. He looks sickly, even with the muscle he's packed on in the last five years. Then again, that might have something to do with the absolutely gigantic bald spot he's sporting on the top of his head. He looks like one of the three stooges, except more ridiculous because of how much his face looks like a neanderthal sculpture that was run over a few times.

"Please have a seat Mr. Mendleton," the guy in the middle of the long table in the front of the room says while pointing at a seat just inside the door I came through. *Great. I get to face him the entire time.*

"My surname is no longer Mendleton," I tell the board. I'm not going to have them let him out on a technicality because they can't keep accurate records.

"We are aware of the change of your name, young man," another member of the board says with a bite in his tone. Fuck. Did I piss them off already? "We are also aware that the attorney for this gentleman here has already been held in contempt for violating your privacy and releasing your name to the press, so we will not speak it for the record, just in case."

Nodding my agreement, I sit down and get sworn in

by the guard who let me in to the room. I wasn't expecting this to be like a mini trial, and my memories of the other times I've been on the stand flash through my mind. My pulse starts to race, and my leg bounces erratically in an attempt to release the sudden rush of adrenaline.

"Are you alright, Mr. Mendleton?"

I look up at the table full of old dudes and struggle to hold back the scathing remark that wants to come out. Swallowing it down takes more effort than I expected, but I close my eyes to picture Mattie.

Mattie loves me. Mattie is waiting for me. No matter what happens today, I won't lose him.

"Super Mattie will always rescue his Sparkles."

I chuckle at the memory of the words Matt whispered in my ear before I went into the waiting room. Opening my eyes, I meet the confused gaze of my monster. At that moment, I realize something. Even if this asshole walks free today, he is a convicted sex offender. He ruined his life when he did what he did to me.

Turning my head to the board, I give them a small smile before answering them.

"Just a small panic attack, gentlemen. I get them from time to time when I experience something that reminds me of the events of that night. For example, I cannot be around root beer or anything that smells like it. Which is a true pity because before that night, I loved old fashioned soda shops and root beer floats. Now, I can't even be around birch trees without hyperventilating."

"Do these attacks happen often? Are they debilitating?"

I spend the next twenty minutes or so answering questions about my various triggers and how the event five years ago has affected not only my quality of life, but my personal relationships as well.

"We've received statements from more than a few individuals that you have had no issues with sexual relationships over the last five years which is part of the reason this gentleman's attorney was successful in getting this hearing. He argued that his client's actions were exaggerated for dramatic effect, as you are on record as being a very flamboyant individual, being employed as a performer in a cabaret type club."

What the fuck? Deep breaths...

Digging my nails into my thighs, I work to calm my breathing before answering. I still can't stop clenching my teeth, but they'll have to deal with that.

"My job has nothing to do with how many dicks have gone up my ass... Shit... Sorry. Please don't hold me in contempt or anything, but I hate being slut shamed. I'm a hypersexual demiromantic and there is absolutely nothing wrong with consensual adults coming together to have some fun as long as it's not deceitful.

"It's true that I have had about twenty times a

plethora of sexual partners since that night. For years, I used sex as a way to punish myself and attempt to rewrite that night in my memory. I was disowned by my family and kicked out, penniless, because I refused to drop the charges against Mr. Dennison and his team-mates. I stood up for myself and was constantly shunned and mocked by the very police and attorneys who were supposed to help me.

"For months, I had constant pressure to turn away and pretend it never happened. But I refused to allow monsters like them to get the opportunity to hurt someone else the way they hurt me. In the end, I was raped by the justice system in a way that destroyed me worse than what Mr. Dennison and his teammates did to me.

"He destroyed my body. He gave me nightmares and panic attacks. But my experience with the police made me fear the people who are supposed to mean safety. They made me feel like it is me against the world and that the world doesn't want me in it."

The members of the board are looking at me like I'm speaking another language, but I push on while they are letting me.

"Sex was my way of taking control of those fears and feelings. What Mr. Dennison and his friends did was outside of my power. After that night, I never had sex that wasn't on my terms. I was ALWAYS in control of every single facet of the interactions, including negoti-ating restraints if I felt I wouldn't be able to physically overpower my partner if I felt even the slightest bit that he could take control. Sex was my outlet when the rest of my life would spin out of control. So, yes, I had a shit-load... Sorry, buttload of sex over the last few years to stop myself from following through on the thoughts that the world would be better off without me in it."

38

MATT

Waiting for Eric to come of the room after testifying is probably the most stressful hour of my life. Spencer and Donnie were both in and out in under twenty minutes. The mousey victim's advocate guy told me each witness testimony is unique when he showed me to this hallway to wait for everyone to be done. But this is ridiculous...

"Barnes?"

Glancing up, I see a man I hoped to never have to encounter again in my life. Rising to my feet slowly, I make sure Andrew Streaker knows exactly what I think of him. Spencer and Donnie stand with me. I feel one of them put a hand on my shoulder, but I don't need the reminder that this isn't the place to start something. I need to be here when Eric is done, not in lockup somewhere.

"What the fuck are you doing here, Streaker?"

He looks genuinely surprised by my anger and takes

a step back. Glancing at the men on either side of me, he sneers at Donnie.

"Fucking snitch, aren't you Hastings?" he snarls and takes a step forward. "How's your luck at finding a bank to give you a loan with that criminal record?"

"I'd rather have my petty record for turning on a bunch of rapists than be rich and let filth like them wander free to hurt others," Don growls out and steps into Streaker's personal space.

Spencer hurriedly pulls us both back as the guards take notice of the aggression and start watching us more closely.

"Thought you had better taste, Barnes. Hanging with a snitch and a fairy boy. Never thought I'd see the day." Turning his attention to my friends, he pushes his luck. "You boys gonna offer up more lies about how the faggot wasn't begging for it that night? Rafe and the guys told me he was a tight little thing. Think they popped his cherry that night?"

Before any of us could launch ourselves at him, the door opens and Eric walks out looking pale and shaky. Pushing away from the guys, I hurry to pull him into my arms, the asshole forgotten for the moment.

"It's over," I whisper to him as I clutch him tighter. "You never have to do this again."

Pushing me back, he gives me a sad smile. "Actually, I'm going to have to do it again in two years. He was denied parole when a few members of the board noticed him getting ... erm... *excited* the more worked up I got."

I am going to ignore that last part for the sake of my

sanity based on the obvious disgust on Eric's face. Grabbing his cheeks, I can't hide my excitement. "He got denied?"

Eric nods as much as my hands will let him and his smile shines like the sun breaking through the clouds. Grabbing him around the waist, I lift him up to twirl him around.

"I'm so proud of you, Sparkles," I tell him when I set him back down.

A snort from behind me pulls my attention back to the asshole who owns the house where this nightmare took place. "You got a problem, Streaker?"

Eric steps around me and looks him up and down while the man is busy staring me down.

"You're Andrew Streaker?" my cutie asks him with a bite to his voice. "*You* are the asshat who owns that crack house rat trap where I was raped?"

"You can't rape the willing," Streaker spits at Eric and I want to throttle him. No one has the right to speak to anyone like that, especially my boy.

Before anyone can move, Eric starts laughing hysterically, holding onto my arm in a vice grip to keep from falling to the floor. I swear it takes minutes for him to stop laughing because every time he seems to get ahold of himself, he looks around the room and cracks up again.

"Come on Sparkles. Let the rest of us in on the joke."

Pointing at Streaker, Eric struggles to get his breathing even enough to speak. "This guy was one of my regular booty calls a few years ago, before I instituted my no repeats rule," he spits out between hiccups.

Streaker starts backing away, shaking his head, but the rest of us are looking between the two of them in confusion. One of the guards looks like he wishes he had some popcorn based on the eager look on his face.

"I didn't recognize him," Eric gasps out as he's mostly back to normal. "I broke off our arrangement when he confessed he loved me and wanted to act out his rape fantasy."

"Did he know your past?" Donnie asks incredulously, but Eric shakes his head in answer.

"It wouldn't have been my first round of CNC, but I didn't do *feelings* with my arrangements. I told him where to find a good dildo," Eric chuckles and waggles his eyebrows. "*I* wasn't the bottom in our arrangement."

Streaker turns whiter than the dress shirt he's wearing before running for the exit. Meanwhile, Eric dissolves back into his uncontrollable laughter. Looking at the other guys, I shrug and hoist my boy into my arms to carry him out. Donnie grabs our coats while Spencer gets the door. The voyeur guard gives me a wink as we walk past, and I shake my head in exasperation.

I figured I would end up with my boy's tears soaking my shirt today. I never expected they would be tears of laughter.

EPILOGUE
ERIC

Two months later:

Going to a pride event with others is a completely new concept for me. Over the last few years, I managed to come either by myself or as part of the show when the Monarch Room was asked to perform or march. Every time I've come, I almost felt like I was obligated to be there just because I'm gay as fuck. I had pride in the life I had built for myself, but I never felt like I belonged among the happy, cheerful throngs of people.

The thing most people don't recognize when it comes to Pride events is that these celebrations are a falsehood for some of us. People on the outside see the colorful outfits, the flashy dancing, and the rainbows and they think that there is no purpose to these parades and celebrations outside of being gay as fuck. Hell, even I didn't understand what there really was to celebrate until this year.

After my first pride when I snuck out at fifteen, each year I come to Pride in the city, I seek out the older guys. I always thought, if anyone would understand why I don't want to celebrate, they would. I heard their stories. I heard about their lovers lost to the AIDS epidemic of the eighties and nineties. They regaled me with tales about their families abandoning them, the forced marriages and children born to satisfy the archaic belief that a man's duty is to procreate...

They faced so much. They lost so much. And yet they are still here forty years later with smiles on their faces, cheering on the younger generations that will hopefully never know their pain and struggle. Those men's stories kept me going many times over the last five years. They survived. They thrived. They gave me the strength to see another tomorrow. From them, I knew that my brighter tomorrow might take years or decades, but it was coming.

Those men saved my life and will never even know it.

This year for Pride in the City, I have the weekend off. I made a managerial decision and closed the Monarch Room so that we can all enjoy the events in the city this weekend. It was tough for Clarence to accept that I wanted to close down completely for the weekend, but with his wedding coming up next month, he doesn't have the time to argue with me when he knows I'm right.

I'm a bit nervous to be here with the rest of the guys from Kink Manor. This is the first time I'm sharing this part of me with them. Mattie was right. It's time I finally open up to them. His coming back into my life helped to slay my dragons and woke up my heart, like a super gay Sleeping Beauty. It's time for my friends to meet the real me and the special men who truly saved me over the years.

"So what are we doing first?" Toby asks, bouncing up next to me. "Do we hit up the food trucks or the stalls? I wanna see if there's anyone selling rainbow collars. Or maybe some light up ears? Oh, they have ice cream?! I want ice cream!"

The excitable pup takes off into the crowd, pansexual flag flaring behind him like the cape he intended it to be. Shiloh looks like he wants to follow, but ultimately huddles into Eli's side. Our kitten doesn't like crowds at all, but he insisted that he wanted to be here, to be a part of this with us. I admire him so much for facing his demons in a healthy way, not like me. I'm glad he doesn't take after me. I think Eli would rip his hair out if he had to deal with another brat in the house.

Not that I'm living in the house anymore. I'm very content with mine and Mattie's little love nest in our trailer at the edge of the woods.

Speaking of Mattie, I glance at my phone to see that I still have quite a while before I get to see him. There was apparently some sort of mandatory staff retreat thing at the University that would be taking up most of the day. For a place that claims to be LGBTQIA+ friendly, Wrenshaw certainly seems to have issues with allowing their staff to be proud to be part of the alphabet mafia.

After a few hours of wandering around the stalls, the rest of the guys decide they want to watch the acts on the stage. The band that is up there now, Heading North, is one that I absolutely adore, and I'm glad to see them furthering their reach. When I first heard their song, Two Steps Away, it was like the words were pulled from my soul. I was glad that Clarence and Felicia agreed to make it the opener to our latest show. We don't perform our Love Yourself show every week, but the club sells out every night we run it.

I'm lost in the music when suddenly, I feel arms wrapping around me from behind. People here are usually better than this. Turning around to teach this neanderthal a lesson, I freeze with my hand in the air. My snarl becomes a thousand watt smile at the sight of my love with a wolfish grin on his face, a face which is painted with the bisexual flag on each cheek.

Throwing both arms around his neck, I pull him to me to plant a kiss on his lips.

"I thought you weren't going to be able to make it today," I say as I step back. "And I see you found the face painter. I'm so proud of you for coming out here."

Matt chuckles and spins me back to face the stage, pulling my back snugly to his front. "I wouldn't miss experiencing this with you for the world. Apparently, no one told the dean that this weekend was Pride in the City. He's pissed that the school missed an opportunity to set up a booth and practically ordered us to come directly down here.

"And the face painter just happens to be a former student so she hooked me up. She told me to let you know that a lot of guys will be jealous that you got me out of my closet first."

"And I will be the *only* guy who gets to experience you if I have anything to say about it," I promise him with a kiss as we turn our attention back to the stage.

We dance and cuddle through all of Heading North's set as well as the next couple of acts. Noticing Bob, one of the older gentlemen that I speak to every year, I pull Matt off to the side of the crowd to introduce them. He's sitting on a wall, fanning himself with a glittery rainbow snap fan when I reach him. Looking behind me, I notice most of the guys from the house have followed us, and I'm secretly happy that my family and friends are going to meet one of the men who made me see that I had a future.

"Bob! What the fuck, man? It's the last day and this is the first I'm seeing you?" I lean down to hug him, noticing he doesn't hug me back as tightly as usual. "Where's Dickie? And Jeff?"

Bob smiles at me, but the light in his eyes is dimmer than I remember from last year. I get the feeling something's not right with my old gays, but I am making a conscious effort to not be so negative inside my head. Perhaps they just had a falling out?

"Dickie is doing well," he says and I feel some of the tension leave me.

"He moved down to Florida this year to be near his sister. You know she's the only one who kept loving him and all that. Well, she broke her wrist taking out the trash back in February, so he moved down there to help her with things. Him being sixty-two to her seventy makes him think he's going to make a big difference or something."

I laugh because it sounds like Dickie. He has some ass backwards logic in his brain sometimes... reminds me of Toby, actually.

Dickie was disowned and beaten by his father when he refused to marry a woman from the church in his early twenties. This was in the early eighties, at the height of the AIDS scare what with Ryan White and everything. According to him, he never officially came out to his family. They all put pieces together and the refusal of the marriage was their proof. His older sister was the only one who even kept in contact with him. In return, he helped her get out of her abusive marriage about a decade later.

I never asked how, but I got the feeling that Sheila isn't a divorcee, but a widow.

"Sounds like him," I say as I sit down on the wall next to my friend. "What about Jeff?"

"How about you introduce me to your friends, Brat?" he counters, blinking rapidly.

Oh, Fuck...

I knew the day would come when I would lose my old guys, but I didn't expect it to be so soon. And Jeff? He was a lot like me. He only shared who he truly was with a select few people, none of which were blood relations. I knew he would take losing Jeremy hard after their forty some years together, but I didn't expect to lose him the very same year. I guess a broken heart really can kill. Looking up at Matt, I give his hand a tight squeeze before turning back to everyone else.

Choking back the tears, I force a smile. Although everyone here would understand, I know Jeff wouldn't want a scene. I get why Bob isn't talking about it. We honor our friend by keeping his wishes. The only scenes Jeff ever wanted made had to be fabulous and fun.

"These guys here are some of my roommates I told you about," I say and introduce everyone individually. "And this hunk of a man here is the love of my life, Lewis Matthias Barnes, the second."

Matt shakes his head in exasperation before reaching out to shake Bob's hand. "Call me Matt, please. This knucklehead loves the fact that my name sounds more pompous than his and yet he is the one with the trust fund."

Bob and the others laugh at our exchange, and I settle in with my head on Matt's shoulder to listen as my old friend shares the tales of his youth with my family. In the middle of one of my favorite stories, Toby comes running up to us with about a dozen kabobs in his hands.

"I bring sustenance for Kink Manor!" he proclaims and shoves his fists out towards Eli and Matt to distribute the food.

"Tobias?" Bob exclaims with more energy than I've seen from him so far today. "What the hell... You're supposed to be in Montana. Does your mother know?"

Toby hides behind Shiloh in a weird Twilight Zone moment of role reversal and shakes his head at my friend.

"Please don't tell her, Uncle Robert," the pup pleads. "I never got on the plane. I knew she wouldn't come here since you live here. Please don't make me go back."

Bob pulls Toby into a forceful hug and weeps onto his shoulder. We all seem to realize those two need a moment, so we head back into the crowd to explore some more before more acts come onto the stage.

After a quick lap around some of the vendor booths with Matt, I pull him back into the crowd in front of the stage to watch the last few acts, sporting fresh face paint and some shiny new pins to make my vest even more fabulous. The world around us completely disappears as we cuddle in the swarm of people. That is, until a very panicked Shiloh comes flying into my arms.

"Shy? Kitten? What happened? What's wrong?"

He's trembling in my arms, but no words are coming. I glance back at Matt to see he is on his phone. Holding Shiloh tightly, I sigh in relief when the music cuts out to signal the changing of the acts.

"...He just came running up to us... No, I don't see him anywhere... Hold on, lemme ask."

Matt crouches in front of me and gently rubs Shiloh's arm to get his attention. It takes a bit, but he finally moves his face out of my chest to look at my love. Matt asks a few yes or no questions to see if we can figure out what is going on.

Were you with Toby before you ran over to us? Yes

Is Toby hurt? No

Did Toby do something to upset you? No

Does Toby know you ran off? Shrug

Did someone touch you? No

"Hey, Kitten, look up at me for a second," I say after the yes and no game has me thinking of something. Shiloh has relaxed a little bit while we were standing here, so he meets my gaze with only a slight hesitation.

"Did you see *Him*?"

Shiloh nods quickly and buries his head back into my chest just as his knees give out. I can feel the vibrations of his screams against my bare chest, but no one can hear his pain over the music. Holding on as tightly as I can, I glance at Matt and the others who are making their way through the crowd to reach us. Making eye contact with Eli, I see the moment he realizes what happened.

"He's out?" Eli mouths, not asking out loud. I just nod and watch as everyone's faces distort with varying levels of rage. Toby goes from horrified to pissed in a matter of seconds, and it's only the fact that Eli is literally holding his leash that keeps him from running off to hunt the bitch down.

"I think it might be time to get the kitten home," Spencer says as the stage is cleared for the final act of the night.

"But Daddy!" Lucky whines, "I wanna watch RealX-Man! He's the whole reason I even agreed to people today!"

I chuckle at the adorable little throwing his version of a tantrum in the middle of the crowd. Even though it's just a bit of foot stomping and pouting, the Lucky we all met last year would never even dream of making even this much of a scene in public, especially while wearing a diaper and a onesie, even if his shorts cover that up.

Glancing down, I see our kitten peek out at our friends with a shy smile. Giving him a little shake, I ask, "Do you want to watch the last show or head out now? It's up to you. The others won't even have to leave. I drove myself so we can bump out in the Mini if you wanna go home to your cave in the basement."

I watch as Shiloh rebuilds himself before our eyes. He has come so very far from the terrified boy that showed up on our doorstep a few years ago. Toby, the loyal pup, reaches out and the two of them hold onto each other's hands as if a hurricane is going to appear just to rip them away from each other.

"Let's stay," Shiloh says with only a slight waver in his voice. "I'm not going to miss a live performance by RealXMan, especially after Toby has been spamming the group chat with all of his Instagram reels. I want to see him perform Rainbow Fam in person, with my own rainbow family."

As the performance starts, I am in awe of how quickly my life has turned around. Snapping a picture of RealXMan's opening outfit, I text it to Clarence as an idea for his wedding dress.

> **Fr3n3my:**
> For the last time, I'm not wearing a dress!
> But yes, that is adorable and Cleo might
> have inspiration for a future act now.

Putting my phone away, I manage to let all of the stress and pain fall back to the background to just enjoy the show. Surrounded by my chosen family and the love of my life, I know that all of my tomorrows are brighter than I could have ever imagined.

ABOUT THE AUTHOR

I am a dog mom living it up in the insanity that is Northeast Ohio. When I'm not documenting the exploits of the characters in my head, I'm either binge reading the works of other amazing authors or losing my voice at hockey games. I'm horribly addicted to coffee, anime, and Asian dramas in addition to building my ever-growing stuffie army.

Kate Bauer is the contemporary alter ego of K.A. Bauer. I guess you could say Kate lives in this reality while K.A. is in a reality where mythical creatures and magic exist, and fate makes finding true love easier. All of her stories are LGBTQIA+ centric, and the characters fight for their rights and happily ever afters.

For the latest news on releases and appearances, check out my website www.authorkabauer.com and sign up for my newsletter.

I can be found on most social media sites under the username @authorkabauer

PET PROJECT

SNEAK PEEK

DONNIE

Did he really just say that?

"What the fuck, Ralph?! What do you mean by that?" I get in his way when he takes a step toward the two men on the floor. "I can admit that Toby here got a little carried away up in the hallway, but you're sounding like you have a problem with something more than him getting in a fight."

"Guys like him are what's wrong with this country!" the security officer shouts as he throws his arm out toward the corner. "They practice sexual deviancies and don't even try to hide them. Their whole house is full of nothing but queers and pedophiles and this sweet young man needs to be away from all of that if he ever wants to be accepted as a normal member of society and not a perverted thug."

Stepping back, I take a protective stance in front of the two men in the corner. I might not have been strong enough years ago to save one boy from my old teammates, but I sure as fuck am able to beat Ralph. I won't let this piece of shit anywhere near these two boys.

"You need to step away, Ralph," I warn him. "For the sake of the years you treated Walt with respect, I'm giving you the opportunity to back out of this peacefully."

The man steps into my personal space to glare at me. "You're just as bad. Turning on your teammates for the sake of some fairy boy. He should have found Jesus and changed his ways. Instead, he just drags others down with him. You both deserve every punishment the Lord brings upon your heads."

The outrage I feel toward the asshole in front of me is about to boil over when a throat clearing pulls all of our attention to the doorway. Matt is standing there, looking absolutely murderous, along with three other faculty members and that Greg guy from the hallway.

"What the fuck did you just say about my boyfriend, Ralph?" Matt snarls and takes a step forward. "Did you seriously just say that he *deserved* to be drugged and gang raped because he's gay?"

Ralph takes a step back from me to look at the people in the doorway. He doesn't even bother to hide his sneer as he looks at Matt before storming out of the room. If I hadn't been right in front of him, I probably wouldn't have been able to stop Toby from going after him. As luck would have it, I somehow manage to catch him up in my arms again when he turns back into a snarling ball of rage.

"I'll take Greg to sign the forms," Professor Michaels

says, pulling the large man with him back toward the desk in the hallway. Professor Silas shakes her head and pulls out her phone.

"Let's get these two somewhere that Toby won't get his ass expelled," Matt grumbles and pats me on the shoulder before reaching down to help Shiloh up from the floor.

SHILOH

"You doing alright, kitten?"

Matt's voice helps to pull me out of the numbness I started to sink into back in the dungeon of the security offices. I felt safe enough with Don, but the security guy always makes me feel a mix of fear and rage that I used to feel around Michael before he almost killed me. It's easiest to go numb around him rather than confront the reason behind the emotions in my experience.

Looking around, I notice we somehow ended up back in the coffee shop and I nod absently. I'm as alright as I think I'm going to get for today. Ever since I saw Michael a few months ago, I have been living on the knife's edge with my anxiety. I didn't realize it was affecting Toby this much as well.

"Where's Toby?" I ask when I notice he isn't next to us. Fear starts taking hold again at the thought of him being taken away from me. My leg starts to shake and breathing is getting harder. I can't lose Toby. I can't ruin his life too.

Matt puts his hand on my leg to stop the shaking and says, "He's in the dean's office giving a statement about the fight and what went down with Ralph, the security guard. He isn't in major trouble and will be back here soon."

"But what about the guy he hit?"

"Greg deserved a good hit to the nuts for what he did to his girlfriend," Matt chuckles and takes a sip of his coffee. "He never should have pretended to be someone else to sleep with her best friend at a party last year. She found out he's been seeing both girls since then, without them realizing."

The wink he gives me makes me smile. My love of melodrama is well known in the house. One of my most vivid memories with Mama consists of our daily dates to watch her soaps. I was too young to really understand what was going on, but I loved to watch her reactions to the insanity on the screen. After she died, it was one of the few ways I had to remember her without feeling pain or fear.

Sipping my hot cocoa, I let the warmth flow into me. It's still too warm outside for hot drinks, but the encounter with the security guard left me feeling cold inside.

"What's going to happen?" I ask in a whisper.

Matt sighs and leans back in his chair.

"Toby will get a warning for violence, but with what happened down in the basement, it will likely be verbal and not even recorded in his file. Greg will hopefully learn to be honest that he wants to be in a poly relationship with his future partners. And Ralph is going to be fired. The cameras in the rooms down there record sound as well as video, so the dean knows exactly what was said. It's a fucking massive understatement to say he is not happy."

I take another sip and ponder over that last part. If that's true, that means everything that has happened down in that place has been recorded. I wonder...

"How long do they keep the recordings before deleting them?" I try for a conversational tone, but judging by the suspicion on his face, I don't think I've succeeded. "Would they still have videos from the summer? Or last year?"

Matt purses his lips but seems to consider it before answering. "I know they regularly hold onto the last ninety days, but I'm pretty sure they have an offsite storage where they keep the older recordings." He narrows his eyes at me before asking, "Why?"

I explain to him the times that I've noticed certain students would get sent there for things like harassment and bullying of the outcasts in the student body, but nothing would ever seem to happen. I have spent a lot of time being invisible, and I notice a lot as a result. There have been a lot of violations to the school code of conduct that have been overlooked just because the perpetrator looks like Toby or Don, especially if the victim is someone who looks like me or is a woman or flamboyant like Eric.

"I'm pretty sure the officer guy threw out the copy of my restraining order as well," I tell him as the door to the shop closes.

"Well, *that* is getting rectified," a voice from across the room calls out, making me jump. I had forgotten we were in a public place. "The safety of all of our students takes precedence over anything else in my university."

Gasping, I duck down to hide behind the curtain of my braids. Why the fuck is the dean talking to me?

MORE BOOKS BY
KATE BAUER

Manor Drive Series

A Little Discovery

Drag Me Up

Pet Project

Teddy Tea Time

Night Shift

No Pain, No Gain

Up/Down Series

Stood Up

Let Down

Trade Up

Down Play

Up For Promotion

Wrenshaw University Series

Freshman Fifteen

Injured Reserve

Professor's Pet

Too Many Men

Dean's List

Frequent Flier

BOOKS BY
K.A. BAUER

ALPHA'S LITTLE PSYCHO SERIES

Alive

Holly Jolly Psycho (Novella)

Unburied

Afraid

Complete Series Omnibus

JAMESON PACK SERIES

Doctor Mate

Fated Mistake

Half Mate

Learned Fate

AFFILIATED STORIES NOT INCLUDED IN SERIES

Fated To Be Free